D1405844

1010230448

LP JAC
JACOBS, T.C.H. (THOMAS CU
RTIS HICKS), 1899-1976
THE TATTOOED MAN

Mystery

Date Due		
24/2/93 William	~~PONDEROSA~~	
16/4/93	~~LOGAN LAKE LIBRARY~~	
16/6/93 Lees	~~SAVONA LIBRARY~~	
MAY 26 1994		
Cooles	KAMLOOPS LIBRARY	
BH		
Hunter		

THE TATTOOED MAN

M.I.5 guessed the identity of the spy who stole the top-secret documents aided by an unknown traitor at the Foreign Office. But Ian Grant, the agent detailed to recover the documents, knew his task was a desperate race against time. For the two Russians fished out of the river by the Thames Police and the Jap tattooist had been murdered the same night. One of the dead men was identified as Peter Herf, the master spy; yet Grant had evidence that he was still alive, and in London.

The C.I.D. were equally anxious to arrest the elusive Herf, and Grant co-operated. From Herf's discarded mistress he got his first real lead. Then it became a violent chase through the treacherous labyrinths of diplomatic immunity, international espionage and the underworld of vice.

*Books by T. C. H. Jacobs in the
Ulverscroft Large Print Series:*

TARGET FOR TERROR
LET HIM STAY DEAD
BLACK TRINITY
THE TATTOOED MAN

THE TATTOOED MAN

by

T. C. H. JACOBS

Complete and Unabridged

ULVERSCROFT
Leicester

First published in Great Britain, 1961

First Large Print Edition
published November 1971

SBN 85456 078 5

© T. C. H. Jacobs, 1961

This special large print edition is
made and printed in England for
F. A. Thorpe, Glenfield, Leicestershire

1

THE TALL MAN thumbed the safety catch of the automatic pistol as he moved with soft, panther-like tread to the door. His companion watched him, his furtive little eyes winking nervously in fearful anticipation. A few moments of tense, almost unbearable silence before he heard the soggy creak of rotten floorboards. He glanced away as the third man appeared from the gloom beyond the open doorway.

"The fog delayed me", announced the newcomer.

The tall man held out his hand and took the long envelope extended to him. He did not examine it, but slipped it into an inside pocket of his overcoat.

"And the girl?" he demanded.

"Safely back."

"All went exactly to plan?"

"Smooth as oil, just like you said. What happens next to the girl?"

"Why do you ask?"

"I've taken quite a fancy to her".

"Forget it, She stays with me."

"So? You're asking for big trouble. She knows too much."

An ugly gleam flickered for a moment in the cold steely eyes. "That's my business."

"Sure. And it could be the business of us all."

"It could be, but it is not."

The newcomer shrugged. "I hope you know what you're doing, because I'm damned if I do. If she rats on us, we've had it."

"She will not talk," declared the tall man with sinister assurance. He slipped a silver brandy flask from his side pocket. "Help yourself to a drink. You've earned it."

"I can do with it, too. The fog's got on m'chest. Phew, it's a stinking mess of a night. Well, here's luck to us all."

He unscrewed the cap and tilted the flask to his lips, gulping the spirit. An expression of distaste contorted his face as he snatched away the flask and stared at it. "What the hell!" he exclaimed. "What muck is this?"

"Good French brandy," said the tall man. "What do you think it is?"

The other did not answer. He staggered

against the table, tried to save himself and dropped with a thud to the floor.

"Observe, my dear Zidkov," said the tall man. "See how swiftly it acts. And it leaves no traces in the body. Yet he is merely unconscious. In twenty minutes he would wake again without feeling the slightest effect or knowing that he had slept. Our scientists are very able men. Come, give me a hand with him."

Zidkov wiped away the perspiration that dripped into his eyes and stooped to grip the ankles. The drugged man was heavy and Zidkov stumbled as they carried him from the room.

Presently Zidkov returned, his long fingers working against his sides in nervous agony, a poor creature of dreadful fear which he fought desperately to control, but could not.

The tall man stepped into the room and held up a hand in a gesture of caution. Zidkov heard the sound of stealthy movement on the stairs. A yellow-faced, slanty-eyed little man muffled in a black overcoat reaching to his ankles and a black hat pulled low over his brow walked in. If it hadn't been for the utter lack of expression in his eyes he would have been a comic little figure.

"It is the fog," he said in a harsh, metallic voice. "You have him ready?"

"Not quite. You may help me, Haiki. The fog has upset our dear friend Zidkov's stomach."

Zidkov moved slowly about the room while they were gone. He *must* make some show of courage or the monster might work on him, too. He waited in a torment of suspense before they returned, bearing between them a corpse which dripped water along the filthy floorboards.

For perhaps forty minutes there was no sound in the room except the snuffling breathing of Zidkov and his restless movements which he tried so hard to control. He did not look at the Jap as he worked. Fear was no strange emotion to him, but never had it churned so sickeningly within him as it did now.

Haiki stopped at last. He began to repack the small, black leather case he had brought. The tall man stood with bent shoulders above the corpse, making a careful examination.

"Yes," he said, "that'll do. Excellent work, Haiki."

"Thank you," nodded Haiki. "It is what you call fool proof."

The tall man drew a bundle of five pound notes from his trouser pocket, peeled off ten and gave them to the Jap.

"I need not warn you, Haiki to keep a silent tongue."

"I understand the virtue of silence." The harsh, metallic voice grated on Zidkov's ears.

When Haiki had gone the tall man turned to Zidkov. His cold eyes looked at him with undisguised contempt.

"Time runs short," he said. "Come, brace yourself. It is quickly now."

Zidkov made a valiant effort to steel himself for the work still to be done. It was not without difficulty that they carried the heavy body down the narrow stairs. Below the stairs a door opened directly on to the riverbank. Half carrying, half dragging the dead man they brought him out.

With a muffled splash the body dropped into the water. Over the river the fog hung like a pall, a dense blanket of reeking dampness that made it impossible to see more than a yard ahead.

"Take my hand," said the tall man. "I

will guide you. I don't want you to fall in, too. That would be a misfortune."

Zidkov felt the powerful fingers close over his wrist. He wanted desperately to snatch his arm away, but he had neither the strength nor the courage.

They moved crab-like along the stone embankment until they came to iron rails. Retaining his hold on Zidkov the tall man hoisted him up and climbed over himself. Zidkov realized a few seconds later that they were walking on wooden planking. He heard a ship's siren hoot dismally in the dense fog and stopped, dragging against the hand which held him so firmly.

"What's wrong?" demanded the other.

"We go the wrong way. This is out into the river, a jetty. I can hear the water swirling against the piles. Listen. Don't you hear it?"

"You are a fool, Zidkov. You allow your imagination to play you tricks like a frightened child in darkness. That is not water you hear. Lean over and listen."

Zidkov, scarcely knowing what he was doing, urged by the contempt and authorty in the other's voice, leaned over the rail. It *was* water, running hard against the jetty piles on a swiftly dropping tide. He knew it was water. It couldn't be anything else.

He was opening his mouth to protest when a pair of muscular arms encircled his waist in crushing pressure, jerked him off his feet and heaved him over the rail. One strangled cry of sheer terror gasped from his lips as he hit the swirling tide and was swept under.

The tall man shrugged. He waited a few minutes before he began to walk back along the jetty, guiding himself by the rail. There was still more work for him to do before his mission was completed. The fog had thrown out his carefully planned schedule, but not too seriously. On the whole it had been lucky, a sure shield against accidental observation.

2

THE LOW BUT singularly penetrating note of the scrambler brought Ian Grant out of deep sleep. There was no time lag. He was immediately wide awake with a brain open for business. As it was the scrambler there was only one place from which the call could be coming. He lifted the telephone "Grant here," he said quietly.

He heard the cold, authoritative voice of his chief, Colonel Mark Borlaise, ordering him to report at once. As he dropped the instrument on its cradle he glanced at his wrist-watch, seven-thirty. It must be something urgent and important for him to be called so early in the morning, especially when he was supposed to be on leave. He wondered vaguely what had blown up during the night.

Grant shaved and dressed with smooth efficiency, all his actions made with a controlled economy of effort, like a well-oiled machine. Twenty minutes later he stepped from his two-seater sports car and crossed the pavement to the offices of The Industrial and Nature Film Corporation.

The interior of the building breathed an early morning, close, unaired smell, overlaid with a suggestion of carbolic. Glass panelled doors on either side of the vestibule were closed and locked. Black stencilled names identified the occupiers as executives of I.N.F.C. Only people like himself knew their real purpose.

He walked through the vestibule to a lift at the rear, concealed behind a heavy door. An attendant was on duty despite the early hour. He looked at him with photographic eyes and said, "Good morning, Mr. Grant. I have instructions to take you right up."

"Thank you, Hobson," smiled Grant. "You're on the night shift I suppose?"

"Come off at nine, sir."

Grant stepped from the lift on the second floor. He waited until it began to descend before he walked along a corridor, doorless, windowless, artificially lighted. At the end a panel in the blank wall slid back and he stepped through. The panel moved silently into place again.

A girl wearing earphones glanced up from a battery of dials and buttons and gave him a smile. "Sorry about this, Ian," she said. "The Old Man is waiting for you. Watch your step. He's steamed up and boiling."

Grant asked: "Any idea what it's all about?"

She shook her head: "Nobody ever tells me anything,"

Grant knew this wasn't true. Jenny Taylor was as much in the Old Man's confidence as anyone could ever hope to be. He wondered then, as he had wondered so often before, why a lovely girl like Jenny should wish for such a life, how, for that matter, she had ever started in it. Jenny gave the lie to those who said that beauty and brains never went together. One day, he thought, he would ask her. She was such a marked contrast to other women with whom he had worked.

Grant said, "Wish me luck," and crossed to the door which looked like oak but was, in fact, steel. Jenny watched him. Six feet two inches of lean, healthy manhood, who wore expensive clothes with a pleasant, engaging untidiness. She knew his age, thirty-three, but his boyish manner and ready laugh made him seem younger, as did a certain eager tilt of his head which reminded her of a young pointer sniffing his first scent. And then you looked again, if you'd been trained that way. You saw the virile power, the lean, watchful vigilance of a man who lived with danger at his heels and swift death just around the corner. You realized the strength of the man, the courage and pertinacity and the agile brain masked by that pleasant, ingenuous exterior. And you liked what you saw. Jenny did.

Colonel Mark Borlaise was talking on the telephone when Grant walked in and closed the door. He signed to him to be seated. The colonel was not above average height, in his late forties, with a lined, leathery face the colour of old parchment, a poker face, hiding thought and emotion. His eyes were the cold grey of the North Sea in winter. Everything about him looked hard and efficient.

He put down the telephone.

"I'm sorry to call you off leave, Grant," he said. "But I need you. What do you know of Morgan Porthy?"

"Only that he's a special secretary to Sir George Bathic. I've never spoken to him."

Borlaise nodded.

"Porthy drove down to Lydd Air Ferry yesterday afternoon. Bathic is in Paris on a secret conference. Porthy was carrying highly confidential documents to him. They were important enough for the F.O. to ask for an escort. I detailed Bruce Sutherland."

"How were the papers carried sir?" asked Grant, as Borlaise paused to light his pipe.

"In Porthy's private brief case. Not in an official case. Porthy and Sutherland arrived at Lydd with half-an-hour to spare. In the airport lounge, while they waited for their names to be called and their flight marshalled, Sutherland went up to the counter to buy two cups of coffee. There was some delay, other customers before him.

"Sutherland kept his eyes on Porthy. He saw a woman come up to him as if she knew him. With her was a man, who remained behind her. He did not speak, neither did she introduce him to Porthy. Sutherland's attention was diverted for a few seconds while he took up the coffee and paid. As he carried the cups to the table the woman walked away, following the man, who was already moving to the exit.

"Porthy volunteered no information as to their identity, although it was obvious he knew the woman. At that moment their names were called over the loudspeaker system. They delayed long enough to drink the coffee before they joined their flight party to go through the formalities.

"They landed at Calais and drove straight to Paris. Porthy opened his case in his hotel bedroom and discovered it contained nothing but a copy of *The Times*. Moreover, it was not his case, but an exact replica, even to a broken stitch in one corner. I've had Bathic himself on to me. He's in a cold sweat. Those papers could bust N.A.T.O. wide open if they fall into Iron Cutain hands. A nasty business, Grant."

"Have they fallen into Iron Cutain hands, sir?"

"Yes."

"Sutherland recognized the couple at Lydd?"

"Yes. He positively identifies the man as Ivan Mikoff. He is pretty sure the girl was Zoya Alexandrovna."

13

"Mikoff! It's all out of character, sir."

"That's what worries me, Grant. Mikoff may not be a top ranking diplomat, but as Cultural Relations Officer he must be fairly well known to a large number of people. He gets around, too. He attends most of the general diplomatic functions. He lectures to all the cracked-brained societies. Porthy must know him well."

"There's no chance that Sutherland could be mistaken?"

"None."

"I don't know the girl, sir?"

"She's supposed to be a nurse-companion to Mikoff's wife. She lives in his house. Sometimes she attends diplomatic functions with him. Our information about her could be better."

"Who suggested the coffee?"

"Porthy."

"Did Sutherland see the couple before she spoke to Porthy?"

"No."

Memory was stirring in Grant's brain. "Hasn't Porthy been in trouble before, sir?"

"Yes. He was at school with Paul Fergus, one of his best friends. When Fergus skipped under the Iron Curtain, Porthy, naturally, was vetted pretty thoroughly. We had no hand in it, but he must have satisfied the F.O. They kept him."

Grant was thinking that Porthy wouldn't be the first mistake they'd made. He asked: "What evidence is there that Porthy knew Zoya Alexandrovna?"

"A fortnight ago he sat next to her at a dinner. Afterwards he danced enough times with her to be noticed. One of our men was there. He reported to me that Porthy seemed smitten by the girl. She is very beautiful, I understand."

"Did he meet her again?"

"I have no evidence that he did."

"As I see it, sir, either Mikoff, or the girl, switched brief cases. To do so with an exact replica shows inside information and very careful preparation. Yet it seems to me that Porthy's mission was in the nature of an emergency which could not have been forseen even by Porthy himself."

"Porthy got his instructions late on Wednesday night."

"So if he's up to any tricky business he had plenty of time. Well, it could be. What'll happen to him?"

"We shall take him apart in small sections, Grant. He will get the full treatment. But if he was a party to the switch it is so crude that I can scarcely believe any man could be such a fool. He knew Sutherland's identity. He knew why he was there."

"He may not have anticipated an escort. On the other hand, he may have felt that the escort provided him with an alibi. What was Mikoff wearing?"

"A loose, Raglan pattern overcoat. It was Mikoff who made the switch. The girl's part was merely to hold Porthy's attention. If Porthy is innocent, then it must have been split second timing, because they would have known that Sutherland was watching."

"Not the sort of skill one would expect in a C.R.O. I can't help feeling, sir, that Porthy will have to talk hard to get himself out of this one."

"I don't care a damn, Grant what happens to Porthy. I want those papers. Now, I'll tell you something I've known for quiet a while, Mikoff is no less a person than Peter Herf."

The information was so startling that

Grant let go a soft whistle of astonishment.

"Herf!" he exclaimed.

"Yes. Rather interesting, don't you think?"

Grant was thinking all right. Peter Herf, the mystery man, the super-spy of unknown origin and nationality, who stole and traded in confidential documents with fantastic success, the man whom every Secret Service officer of the Western nations had vainly sought to trap for the past ten years or more.

The telephone rang. Borlaise answered. Grant watched him. He saw the thin lips tighten and an icy gleam in the grey eyes. Borlaise said. "Thank you. I'll contact you."

He put the instrument down, keeping his hand upon it. The silence in the room was electric. Presently he said: "The Thames Police have fished the body of Peter Herf out of the water at Woolwich. He was drowned some time during the night."

"Good God!" exclaimed Grant. "That's an odd way for such a man to die! And why Woolwich?"

The telephone shrilled again. Grant

listened to a brief, one sided conversation before Borlaise rang off.

"Did you get that ?" he asked.

"Not all of it sir."

"Herf, in his identity of Mikoff, attended a tea-party given by some idiot society calling themselves 'The Daughters of Liberty' and was with them, talking to them, at the exact time Porthy was being robbed at Lydd. What the hell, Grant! What the hell! That was McLean reporting. He wouldn't make a mistake. Neither would Sutherland. Obviously there has been an impersonation. The point is, which one was Herf? And does it matter? The plan succeeded."

"The body at Woolwich would have been identified as that of Mikoff, sir. How was it identified? By papers in his pocket?"

"Yes, in the first place I suppose. No doubt the police have checked with the embassy, too. I know what you're thinking. It's easy to stick papers in a man's pocket before you drown him. According to the police he must have walked off the river embankment in the fog. He was wearing a heavy overcoat and wouldn't stand much chance. The tide was falling fast when he went in. I'm waiting now for Sutherland. You'd better wait, too. He's on his way from London Airport, alone. Bathic is keeping Porthy in Paris. When you've listened to Sutherland's story you must get over to New Scotland Yard and contact Chief Superintendent John Bellamy. Then go down to Woolwich, see the body and get the whole details."

"Have we positive means of identification as Peter Herf, sir?"

"Yes, finger-prints, and an eagle tattooed on his right fore-arm. Bellamy has him on the list of foreign criminals who might visit the country. There's not likely to be any doubt about his identity."

"Who obtained the finger-prints?"

"The Dutch police, some years ago."

"May I ask, sir, how you first became aware that Mikoff and Herf were the same person?"

"He was being shown over the Ford works at Dagenham. He got some paint on his sleeve and hand. He took off his jacket to be cleaned and went into the lavatories to wash his hand. McLean was one of the party. He followed him. He saw the tattooed eagle and reported it as additional information, not knowing the significance. But I did. I've checked back. Mikoff is Herf, all right."

"Have we checked on finger-prints?"

"No."

"So there might be just the bare possibility . . . "

"No, Grant. His description fits too exactly with that supplied by the Dutch. Anyway, if the finger-prints of the corpse tally, then there's not a shred of doubt. What's your worry?"

"I am impressed by the casual, accidental nature of the whole affair. If Porthy was not in collusion . . . "

"If Porthy was not in collusion, then it shows exceedingly good up-to-the-minute information which is very disturbing, Grant."

"But the exact duplicate of Porthy's private brief case, sir."

"Yes, I know. It's a hard one to crack. They had that brief case already prepared. If it hadn't happened yesterday it would some other time. Porthy was either in collusion, or has been selected as a likely proposition. It shows organisation of a very high order."

"Assuming Porthy is innocent, sir."

"Yes. You don't think he is. Neither do I. But we have to work on the assumption that he is. This is something that has to be settled swiftly, Grant. We have to stop those papers before they go out of the country. Photographic copies would be bad enough. But they could be denied. You can't deny the actual documents, or the P.M.'s signature."

A red light flickered over the door and a buzzer purred. Borlaise depressed a button on his desk. The door opened and Bruce Sutherland stepped in. He closed the door and turned to face them. Grant saw the lines of fatigue in his lean face. He felt very sorry for him. It was something which might have happened to a much more experienced man than young Sutherland.

3

CHIEF SUPERINTENDENT JOHN BELLAMY was the youngest man ever to have held such senior rank in the Metropolitan Police. He was as tall as Grant and not unlike him in appearance. Grant had met him for the first time some six months ago, and liked him.

He pushed a box of cigarettes across the desk. Grant took one and Bellamy flicked flame to his lighter.

"What exactly do you want to know?" he asked. "Colonel Borlaise phoned that you were coming over, but he gave me no details. It's about Mikoff, isn't it?"

"Yes. I want all the information you have."

"I can give you that. But Superintendent Barnard is dealing with the Woolwich business. I have only brief details. Mikoff, of course, is Peter Herf. We've been after him for years."

"Herf is suspected of stealing Foreign Office papers."

"That's his speciality. But he's not above other criminal practices. Or was. He's dead now. Rather a queer affair. On the evidence one must assume that he died accidentally. But I'm not so sure. He was the wrong type to go out that way."

"That is how I feel," agreed Grant. "What was he doing on the river bank in a thick fog? When did he die? Has that been established?"

"Roughly, yes. One can never be too accurate about it. From the preliminary medical evidence he died between nine o'clock and midnight. As far as that goes it reveals nothing but plain drowning. No marks, or suggestion of poison, nothing to point to violence. But according to the river men who found the body there's never more than four feet of water at that point."

"He could have fallen in at some other point and been carried there."

"No, the river men are emphatic that he went in at the place where he was found. There's a mud bank and a back eddy which makes it a certainty. The first thought that occurred to me was that the body was meant to be found so quickly. Someone knew all about the way that back eddy worked."

"And Herf was murdered?"

"Yes."

"Then the medical evidence would show an absence of water in the lungs."

"If he was dead when he went in. He wasn't dead. He was alive and breathing. That is important to you, I feel."

"How?" asked Grant, seeing quite a number of possibilities, but wishing to know Bellamy's ideas.

"If Herf was connected with the theft and you suspected him, what would be your conclusions if shortly afterwards he was found drowned, apparently by mis-adventure?"

"And no papers on his body? I suppose we should conclude that the papers were somewhere hidden, probably in his house, or that they had already been passed on. We should do our best to trace them, even though he is covered by diplomatic privilege. All our agents everywhere would be alerted and the whole machinery brought into swift operation. If we didn't get quick success we should know he'd beaten us to it."

"Then you'd sit back and wait for the

storm, eh? I know. I've had some. All the evidence we have points to death by accident. If, however, you discover that some person closely connected with Herf is missing, or going abroad in the near future, then you may have some guide."

"The papers could go out in the diplomatic bag."

"If they are important and urgent they are more likely to go by hand, by special messenger. You are assuming that Herf was working for the Russians when he stole the papers?"

"Yes, indeed. Who else?"

"Herf has always been a free lance. We know little enough about him, but we do know that he's a remarkably fine linguist and a master of disguise. He may have thrown in his lot with the Russians. There must be a reason why they let him over here as Mikoff, their C.R.O. But I'd bear in mind that Herf was an exceedingly slippery customer and as likely to double-cross Russians as anyone else."

"Herf has never been through British hands?"

"No. Most of our information comes from the Dutch."

"And finger-prints, I understand?"

"Yes."

"They tally?"

"Yes. That's how we identified him. He's on the index."

"Tell me something about his history."

Bellamy took a file from the desk drawer. He turned over several pages before he said: "This is his record as far as we know it. There's a hell of a lot missing. We don't know his real name or where he comes from. He first came under the notice of the Dutch police some fifteen years ago. He was then in his early thirties. He was suspected of issuing counterfeit money, the dropper for an international gang. He managed to give the police the slip and escaped from Holland. A year later there was a daring series of bank robberies in France and Belgium, all running to the same pattern. The thief was eventually seen and described by a French detective, who caught him red handed, but failed to arrest him. Herf shot him with an ingenious contraption of a spring gun concealed in his jacket pocket. The officer was wounded, but not too seriously. Through Interpol, the description was linked with Herf.

"Some while later there was a theft of confidential documents and a large sum of money from American H.Q. in West Germany. One of their agents was smart enough to trace the thief, a man employed as a chauffeur to a general. The man was arrested as he crossed the Dutch frontier. His finger-prints proved him to be Herf. The Americans turned him over to the Dutch for trial on the original charge. But Herf vanished from his prison cell. It was the complete disappearing trick. The cell door was locked, but Herf was not there. The lock had not been tampered with and there was nothing to indicate how he had broken out."

"One of the guards," suggested Grant.

"It must have been, but no one was accused. What I know of the Dutch they'd have been very thorough in their investigation. Herf's finger-prints cropped up several times during the next ten years. In France, Denmark and in Switzerland. Most of the crimes were robberies or blackmail. And now he has turned up in London as a member of the Russian Embassy staff. It's very odd. How long has he been over here?"

"Nine months. By the way, you didn't mention the tattooing on his forearm."

"Tattooing? There's nothing in our records. He must have had it done since."

Grant was thinking that there was less in police records than in those of his own department. Bellamy's records covered only Herf's criminal ventures. Except for the incident of the Americans it made no reference to his espionage activities. Well, one wouldn't expect it. The Secret Services do not enlist police aid unless they have to. Even then they keep their secrets.

"I'll give you a note to Barnard if you like," volunteered Bellamy. "You'll probably find him at the Woolwich station. I'll give you all the help I can, Barnard is the man in charge."

A knock sounded on the door. In response to Bellamy's invitation a uniformed constable entered. He laid an official slip upon the desk. "Just come in, sir," he announced, and withdrew.

Bellamy said: "It looks to me, Grant as if you are in for quite a busy time. Do you know Nikola Zidkov?"

"Yes. He's another of the embassy people."

"Was, Grant. His body has just been recovered from the river, caught up in the piles of a wharf. You could stop at Blackwall on your way down. Inspector Gregory of the Thames Division will have the details. I'll telephone him and say you are coming."

"I'm very much obliged," said Grant.

As they shook hands Bellamy said: "Herf was essentially a free lance, a lone wolf. I find it hard to credit him working for anyone else, however much they paid him. You might find a lead in that thought. The criminal mind doesn't often change."

Grant went out to his car and drove eastwards to Blackwall.

Inspector Gregory was rather short for a policeman, with a weather-beaten face and loud voice, as if he spent his time bellowing against high wind.

"Where did you pick up the second body?" asked Grant.

"Not so far from the first. He got entangled in some old chains around the piles of a wharf. There's a derelict jetty downstream. I reckon they both walked over in mistake during the fog. It was a real pea-souper last night. You can't be sure where you're walking when you've got that around you."

"Would they get on the jetty straight from the quay?"

"It's not a quay. It's a kind of stone embankment at the rear of some buildings. Way back it used to be a hide and skin store. But it's been more or less empty for years. Scheduled for demolition, when they get around to it."

"Could they reach the jetty without going through the buildings?"

"Yes, they could, if they knew how. What the hell they were doing trespassing along there at that time of night beats me. And how they fell in. There's still a good sound rail along the jetty."

"How does the finding of the second body square with your estimate regarding the first? Where he went in, I mean."

"It squares all right. One went over the land end and the other over the river. They must have gone in within a few minutes of each other. The first slipped and fell. The second got into a blind panic and ran the wrong way."

"There was still the rail," Grant reminded him.

"Yes, there was. But there's no account-
ing for the actions of a man in a panic.
Like suicides. You never know what they'll
do, sir."

That might well be true. But Grant
didn't think it had happened that way. He
had no reasons. It was just a hunch.

He drove on to Woolwich, using the
river tunnel.

4

GRANT LOCATED Superintendent Barnard at the Woolwich police station. He had never met him, but he knew him by sight and was aware of his high reputation as a detective.

Barnard was said to be a difficult, ill-tempered man, intolerant of failure, driving men to the limit of endurance. But he never asked any man to do what he was not prepared to do, or had not done, himself. If his subordinates disliked him, at least they respected him.

Grant handed him Bellamy's note.

Barnard read it, gave him an unfriendly stare of his hard eyes, summing him up in swift appraisal.

"I am instructed to give you assistance," he announced as if he hated the idea. "What do you want?"

Grant had the feeling that he wasn't going to like Barnard very much.

"My department finds it surprising that a man of Herf's character and experience should die the way he did. We are anxious to have all the information you are able to give us, together with a sight of any papers found on the body."

"There were no papers, except an identity card issued by the Russian Embassy. My reports will, no doubt, be made available to you."

"The matter is very urgent, Superintendent."

"I see. Very well. Dr. Silver, the pathologist, has just completed post mortems on the two bodies. I have nothing more than that at present."

"With what results?"

"Rather surprising, Mr. Grant. Zidkov was drowned in the river. Herf was not."

Grant stared at the grim-faced superintendent.

"Would you please explain?" he requested.

"Zidkov's lungs were full of Thames water, thick with oil and mud. Herf's lungs contained tank water, with heavy traces of rust. Herf was dead when he was thrown into the river. Zidkov was very much alive. How would you account for that?"

"I can't. Do you suspect Zidkov murdered Herf?"

"I think it highly improbable."

"Well, what then?"

"Zidkov was too small and lacking in the strength necessary to carry, or even drag, such a big man as Herf, much less drown him in a tank, even if he was unconscious."

"So he must have had assistance."

"Either he assisted in the assassination and dumping of Herf in the river, or he was fleeing in panic from the assassins. With the tide sweeping down in full ebb, clad in a heavy overcoat, he would have had not a dog's chance, even if he were a strong swimmer."

"No one heard any screams?" asked Grant, and wished he'd kept silent.

"Screams would not excite attention in this neighbourhood, Mr. Grant. In any case, you flatter me. I have still to begin my investigation. I would ask if you have any private information which you are permitted to reveal to a mere policeman that you will confide it to me. This has all the hall marks of a very dirty case, which, I assume, you desire solved as much as I may do."

Barnard was speaking professionally. He meant a case which was going to present unusual and difficult problems and a great volume of sheer hard work for the police.

"All I can tell you is that Herf is suspected of stealing confidéntial Foreign Office documents " replied Grant.

"When and how ?"

"Yesterday afternoon. He lifted them from a Foreign Office messenger at Lydd Airport. Beyond that, we have no information bearing on this drowning."

"Very careless of the Foreign Office messenger, if I may say so Mr. Grant."

"I don't know the details."

"But you know Herf's record ?"

"Mr. Bellamy has put me in the picture."

"So I understand. What do you want to do now ?"

"Inspect the bodies."

"Very well. Dr. Silver is having Herf's body removed to St. Cross hospital for more detailed examination."

"Does that mean he is not sure of the cause of death ?"

"Not at all. He is quite sure. The cause of death in both cases was drowning. There is no doubt about that. But Herf was a very powerful man. There are no marks of violence on the body, beyond a very slight bruising."

"You couldn't drown a man like that in a tank without him taking great exception to the treatment. So he was either drunk, or drugged."

"There are no traces of alcohol sufficient to suggest he was drunk. If he was drugged, a chemical analysis will reveal the nature of the drug and probably how it was administered, even some suggestion as to its origin. The more unusual, the better chance of tracing of course. All right, come with me."

Grant followed the superintendent to the mortuary. A uniformed constable opened the door. The mortuary keeper drew back the sheet covering one of the bodies.

Barnard said, "Herf."

Grant looked down at the dead body of the man who had been such a chronic headache to so many security forces. His face in death was pale and sallow. His features were good almost aristocratic, his lips thin and his jaw strong. In his youth he must have been quite handsome. His head was of a squareness usually associated with

Germans. On his right forearm a spread winged eagle was tattooed in blue and red. It was about two inches in wing span, its perfection of detail obviously the work of an expert. It showed a faded appearance as if it were some years old. Grant studied it closely. He had a feeling that he ought to recognize this particular design, but he could not. It was difficult to assess the dead man's age, but he thought it would not be less than the late forties.

He straightened up. "Thank you," he said, and turned away, "I would very much like a photograph of the tattooing, Mr. Barnard."

"You recognize it?"

"I feel I ought to, but I don't."

"You'd better look at Zidkov, too." Barnard signed to the mortuary keeper, who drew down the sheet.

Grant recognized the mean, furtive face of the Russian. The man had died in an extremity of fear. When he remarked on it, Barnard nodded:

"Yes, something scared him. His death could have been the result of his terror."

"Did he carry papers?"

"Yes. The identity card, similar to Herf,

37

and several letters, badly damaged by water. I've sent them to the laboratory for drying and examination. Photographic copies will be available shortly. Well, if you're satisfied we'll return."

They were entering the station again when a quick step sounded behind them. Grant recognized the burly man in a bowler hat and shabby mackintosh, Detective Inspector Trotter, a merry-eyed old timer of the C.I.D. reputed to be the only officer who could work amicably with Barnard, simply because he didn't care a damn for anyone, high or low, a natural attitude of mind reinforced by a small private fortune inherited from an old aunt whose sole kin he had been.

"Well, look who's here!" exclaimed Trotter, extending a great ham of a hand. "So we've got the cloak and dagger boys, too! As if we hadn't enough trouble. How are you, Mr. Grant?"

"Fine," said Grant, withdrawing his hand before it was completely mangled. He formed the impression that Trotter didn't know his own strength. He ought to have been more cautious. It had happened the last time they met.

Barnard said, impatiently: "Well, Trotter?"

"Sure, Super, we've located it. It's in the old house on the riverbank, like you said."

"All right. I'll see the place."

"Would I be in the way?" asked Grant.

"No," said Barnard grudgingly. "I suppose you'd better see it, too. But I must ask you not to touch anything."

"I'll keep my hands in my pockets."

Trotter gave Grant a merry wink and a grin as they followed the superintendent to the police car.

"How's the spy business?" he asked.

"Flourishing."

"Looks like they've got around to knocking each other off. It'll save you work if they keep on at the game. You can pass the buck to the poor half-witted cops, eh?"

"Don't talk like a fool, Trotter," snarled Barnard.

"Sorry, Super. Just my fun."

Barnard made a growling noise in his throat and got into the car. Grant got in beside him. Trotter slid into the driving seat and the car glided smoothly from the yard.

5

THE HOUSE WAS right on the river bank, in an area scheduled for clearing. It might once have been the residence of a merchant captain, with a nice garden, and lawns and a sandy beach. But that was a very long time ago.

Trotter led the way along a narrow embankment, with the dark, oily waters of the Thames lapping against it. A jetty, some thirty feet long, stuck out into the river, supported on wooden piles, old and rotten. It was one of several Grant could see as he looked downstream, all apparently near derelict.

"That's where they fished Herf out of the water," said Trotter. "There's a mud bank out there which makes this bit of the river more or less a pool, a back eddy, or something, that prevented the body being carried downstream."

"And Zidkov?" asked Grant.

Trotter pointed to the next jetty.

"Under that one. If he hadn't got caught

up in the chains he'd probably be down off Gravesend by now."

Grant looked at the dark water. He was thinking of what Borlaise had said. Whoever put Herf's body in at this particular spot knew something about the way the water flowed.

Trotter voiced his thoughts.

"Looks like Herf was meant to be discovered. But Zidkov not."

He turned and pushed open a door behind them. Barnard stepped into the gloomy interior, smelling strongly of stale fruit and vegetables, coupled with the rank odour of decay.

Trotter said: "The front rooms are used by the barrow boys, Super. They store their stuff here and aren't particular about their rubbish. Years ago the place used to be a hide and skin store. There's a lot of muck left from that, too."

A uniformed constable stood in what had once been a fine hall. A large, arched door, the original front entrance, stood open, letting in enough light for them to see the broad stairs and the hall floor, littered with vegetable refuse. Doorways on either side gaped like dark cave mouths.

The constable saluted Barnard.

"A street trader has been here, sir. I refused him admittance. He wants some of his stock."

"He must wait. Has he any right to use this place as a store?"

"Not as far as I know, sir. But it has been the custom for as long as I've been on this beat. Nobody has objected."

"I see. Well, he must wait."

Barnard began to mount the stairs, which creaked beneath his weight. Plaster hung from the filthy walls and lay crushed on the wooden treads. He paused several times to flash his torch. Some of the plaster looked to Grant as if it had been quite recently trodden into the wood.

On the second floor landing Barnard paused. Trotter came up beside him and shone a torch into a doorless room with a sloping ceiling, evidently right under the roof. The torchbeam shone on the rusty tank, built into the wall. A pipe ran into it from a point higher up the wall.

"Filled by rainwater," announced Trotter. "It must be sixty years old, if it's a day."

In the light of the torch Grant saw the

heavy layer of dust on the floor, and the wet marks where pools of water had gathered around the tank. A line of drips led out to the landing, sinister evidence of what had happened.

Barnard said "Stay there, Mr. Grant," and stepped in, moving cautiously towards the tank. He flashed his torch over the outer surfaces and into the tank. When he came out again he wore a rather thoughtful expression. "The tank will have to be filtered and emptied, Trotter. Samples of the water must be taken, too. Get in touch with Dr. Lucas. It's his job, not ours."

Dr. Lucas, Grant knew, was the director of the police laboratory a very able scientist who had a great number of successes to his credit.

Trotter pushed open a door to their left and shone his torch into the room. Barnard added his own torchbeam. The window was boarded up. A long, deal table stood in the centre, with a couple of plywood tea chests and a cane seated chair without a back. In a corner was a camp bed with a pair of tattered grey army blankets thrown in an untidy heap upon it. The hearth of a rusty fireplace was littered with cigarette ends.

There was wood ash in the grate that looked comparatively new.

It was the table which interested Grant, and the floor around and beneath. Traces of water showed on the table top. On the floor the dust and grime of ages had been churned into mud. Spots of grease on the table indicated where three candles had burned themselves out.

Barnard stood with his torch beam sweeping over the table and floor. He said presently "The body was brought in here and laid on the table. Why?"

"They were waiting for the tide to fall, Super."

Barnard turned his head slowly and looked at Trotter.

"Thank you, Trotter. Perhaps you can tell me why they waited so long and why it was necessary for someone to stand and walk around the body during that time?"

Trotter was not in the least daunted by the heavy sarcasm in the slow, deliberate voice of the superintendent. He said, cheerfully:

"Maybe, making sure he was dead, Super. There's something damned queer about the whole business. It doesn't add up."

"No. Such as?"

"Well, damn it, murderers are usually mighty eager to hide their bodies."

"These may have been."

"If they had been they'd have carried him out to the end of the jetty and dropped him into deep water. Somebody has been using this room for quite a time, sleeping here. He probably knew all about the peculiar set of the tides just below us."

"So?"

"Not only did they want the body found, but they wanted it found quickly. The workmen from the dust destructor use that embankment as a short cut. The first one along this morning would have seen the body. It's only a chance that the river boys found Herf first."

"How do you know?"

"The constable down below. I talked to him."

"So on your reasoning the man who has been using this room was a party to the murder."

"Why not?" said Trotter. "Most of those cigarette ends over there are foreign, French, I'd say. There's three or four with cardboard tubes, Russian. Tramps don't smoke those sort of cigarettes, Super."

Barnard gave him an icy stare.

"We shall know more about that, Trotter when we find the man. Now, Mr. Grant are you satisfied?"

Grant was being dismissed.

"I'd like samples of those cigarette ends," he said. "I might be able to match them."

"Samples will be reserved for you, Mr. Grant. But they must have saliva and finger-print tests first."

"Thank you," said Grant. "I'm still puzzled as to why the body was laid on the table and not left on the floor, as one would have thought. He was a heavy man."

"I am puzzled, too, Mr. Grant. No doubt, in time, we shall find the answers."

Time! That was one thing of which Grant was short. But it was plain that he was no longer welcome, or likely to learn much else.

"I'll walk up with you," said Trotter.

"I want Ostler, Jones, Morgan and a full crew down here at once," ordered Barnard. "Then telephone Dr. Lucas. I want all the men who have been on this beat in the past twelve months, too. And emergency lighting

46

equipment. In the meantime, I'll stay here."

"Very good, Super."

Outside the house they found the street trader arguing with another uniformed constable. Trotter said to him: "Sorry, chum, but you've had it for today. So you'd better hook it."

"What about my stuff all going rotten in there? I can't afford to lose——"

"You shouldn't have put it there."

"Why not? I pay rent for it, don't I?"

"Do you?"

"Certainly I do. Five bob a week to Haiki Yuma, the Jap, up there at the antique shop. He owns this place."

Trotter looked at the constable, who shrugged his shoulders.

"First I've heard of it, sir. The house is scheduled for demolition, same as all the rest. I thought the Council had taken it over."

"How long have you been paying the Jap rent?" demanded Trotter.

"Years."

"Has the man who's been sleeping here paid rent, too?"

"I wouldn't know. He's a queer 'un. Comes and goes."

"What's his name?"

"Search me. He's a foreigner. I've never spoken to him."

"What does he look like?"

"Big man, about fifty. Maybe a German. We don't ask no questions down here, guv."

"Good looking chap, pale faced, going grey over the temples?"

"Yes, something like that."

"Has he got any friends?"

"Not that I know of. I reckon not. He's a surly type. Don't speak to anybody. He was here last night."

"How do you know?"

"I saw him in Hare Street."

"In the pea-souper fog?"

"Yes, under a lamp. I recognized him, even if I didn't see him very clearly. He's got a way of walking, kind of stiff legged. He was making this way. Where else would he be going?"

"Where indeed?" said Trotter. "Any idea what he does for a living?"

"I told you, guv, we don't ask questions. But I wouldn't be surprised if you ain't got his dabs."

"Like that, eh?"

"I reckon so."

"What's your name, chum?"

"Sam Smelly, and don't get funny about that either."

Trotter grinned. He said to the constable: "Let him take out what he wants. You can tell Mr. Barnard I said so."

"Thanks guv," said Smelly. "You're a gent."

"I may want to talk to you again, chum. If you hear anything about that foreigner I want to know it. Understand?"

"Yes, sure. I'll have a nose round."

Trotter and Grant walked up the slope and came to the broad approach to the Free Ferry.

"Are you in a hurry?" asked Trotter.

"Not if there's something more to be learned. Why?"

"I think we could take a look at Mr. Kaiki Yuma. But I must get the finger-print boys and photographers along first, and fix it with Lucas."

"All right," agreed Grant. "I'll walk up and locate the antique shop. I think I saw it as I drove down. It's just around the corner up here."

"Don't do any cloak and dagger stuff," grinned Trotter, "or you'll get me sacked."

6

GRANT FOUND THE shop where he had anticipated it would be. He walked slowly past it on the opposite side of the street. From this distance he could not see into the interior of the shop. The single window revealed a remarkable collection of old junk, odds and ends of furniture and one enormous oil painting of impossible cliffs battered by an equally impossible sea. He wondered idly who could have painted such a monstrosity and who would buy it. Perhaps it was there to attract attention to the window.

He crossed the road higher up and came down on the shop side. Outside, he stopped to peer in under pretence of viewing the junk. It was too dark to see anything. Making up his mind, he tried the door handle and found it locked.

A road sweeper was coming up the street pushing a dust cart, Grant stopped him.

"Do you know when this shop opens?" he asked.

"Ain't it open? Well, it generally is. It's kept by a Jap."

"I know. I want to see him."

"Sorry, mister. I ain't seen him."

The road sweeper went on. Grant eyed the side door. He was in the grip of one of his hunches. Illogical, maybe, but he had found it never paid to ignore them. He looked for a bell and found none.

The door had a knob below the Yale lock. He put out his hand and gently turned. He was not particularly surprised when the door opened. Beyond the door a flight of stairs led straight up from the street, wooden stairs, carpeted in threadbare red fibre.

Grant closed the door, softly, and began to mount. He went very slowly, listening. He heard a whisper of sound within the house. On the landing he paused. There were three doors, all closed. He tried the first and found it locked. The second was not. He knocked gently and waited. Nothing happened, so he opened the door.

A warm wave of air laden with a peculiar scent wafted out to him from the darkened room. Grant sniffed. Opium, but stale. He said, quietly: "Is anybody at home?" Then his groping hand found the electric switch. The light came on, softly shaded, glowing over a room beautifully and expensively furnished in Oriental style.

Mr. Haiki Yuma sat comfortably on a couch of silk tapestry. An opium pipe lay on the floor, just beyond reach of the hand which hung limply down. No wonder Haiki Yuma had not responded. He was dead. In the centre of his forehead was a ragged little red-rimmed hole and a tiny trickle of blood had dried hard on his nose and chin, dividing his yellow face in neat halves.

Grant stood in the doorway starring at the dead Jap. Haiki Yuma had been in the Land of the Poppy when that bullet had struck him, which suggested that his assassin was familiar with his habits, but could have been just lucky. Whatever the motive for the murder, it certainly was not robbery. The room was loaded with valuable pieces, some so plainly of gold and precious stones that any thief would have recognized their value.

Haiki Yuma was clad in an Oriental dressing-gown with a black collar and cuffs and an elaborate floral design in green, gold and blue. A black jacket and overcoat were thrown across a chair. A soft black hat lay on the floor beside them.

Grant stepped in, watching the floor, careful not to tread on anything which might be lying there. He took up the overcoat and went through the pockets. They were empty. When he lifted the jacket he saw the black leather case beneath.

The jacket pockets contained a knife, cheap Japanese lighter, a crushed packet of cigarettes, and a few trade cards bearing his name and address, nothing else. Grant laid it down.

Very carefully he tried to open the leather case without leaving any finger-prints upon it. He had gloves, but they were thick leather. In the end he had to put them on and try again. The case had a trick catch which he had met before. He eased it open and discovered that it contained a number of peculiar instruments and needles, together with several small bottles of coloured fluids and a dirty piece of rag, heavily stained.

It was several moments before he recognized them for what they were, tattooing instruments. Old fashioned, nonelectrical types of the variety still extensively used in the Far East.

He closed the case again, returned both coats to their original position and stole soft-footed from the room. That peculiar additional sense he had developed over the years told him that he had made a discovery of vital importance, but at the moment he had only the glimmer of an idea what it was, an idea so improbable that he dismissed it almost at once.

He waited outside the shop for ten minutes before Trotter appeared, a big burly man looking as if he could punch holes in a stone wall.

Trotter said: "Well?"

"Not so well," replied Grant. "You've got another corpse on your hands."

"Haiki Yuma?"

"Yes."

"All right, don't make me a nervous wreck waiting for the news. Where is he?"

"Upstairs."

"I told you not to——"

"The door was open. I regarded it as an invitation. I haven't touched anything. He's been dead a good many hours."

"Let's go and see."

Grant led the way up the stairs. He had left the electric light burning. Trotter stood in the doorway taking in the scene. Then he walked over and examined the wound.

"Shot at close quarters. There's powder blackening. I suppose he was flat out with opium smoke." He looked around the room. "What a place! Aladdin's Cave, or was it Ali Babba? Old Barnard's going to be jumping mad with this. What a turn-up! Don't forget, *I* found him."

"You're welcome," smiled Grant. "The three deaths must be connected, Trotter. It's too much of a coincidence otherwise."

"It does happen, you know."

"Yes, but not here."

"I must say it looks like you said. Well, I wonder if you'd mind going down and telling Barnard. There's a lot of work to be done here, too. Just tell him gently. Are you coming back?"

"No. Has Herf's body been removed yet?"

"Yes. Dr. Silver is going to work on it at his hospital, St. Cross Why?"

"I thought I'd like another look at it. But it doesn't really matter."

You're thinking that Sam Smelly's description could fit Herf?"

"Yes, so did you."

"What do you make of it?"

"Damned queer. You might have a rough time ahead, but so have I. I'll keep in touch."

"Anything I can do, you know. Glad of it."

Grant walked back to the riverside. He found half a dozen C.I.D. men there with Barnard. Grant said to him: "Trotter would like you to come up to the antique shop. Haiki Yuma, the owner, was shot dead during the night. According to one of the barrow boys, Yuma owns this house and collects rent for storage."

"So?" said Barnard, softly. "Very well, I will come with you. Who found the body, you or Trotter?"

"Trotter. I merely wanted a sight of the Jap in case I knew him. I was waiting outside the shop, which was closed. But the side entrance was open. So Trotter went up. I followed."

Barnard said nothing, but he looked grim. Outside the shop he said, "Thank you, Mr. Grant," and opened the side door, closing it behind him. Grant smiled to himself as he walked back to the police station, where his car was parked. He hoped he wouldn't have to see too much of Barnard.

He drove as fast as he dared through Greenwich, Deptford, New Cross to London Bridge. Dr. Silver was just preparing to leave when Grant walked into the Pathology Department at St. Cross Hospital. He introduced himself as a colleague of Superintendent Barnard.

"I've just had another call from Woolwich," said Silver.

"A straightforward shooting case Doctor. A Jap, named Yuma. It's probably connected with the other two. If I may keep you a moment, I want to ask some questions on tattooing."

"Tattooing?"

"Yes. Mikoff's right arm is tattooed."

"An eagle, an expert piece of work."

"Have you examined it closely?"

"No, I merely noticed how good it was. Why?"

"Is it possible to tattoo a dead body?"

Silver gave him a curious stare: "Yes. Post-mortem tattooing is a frequent occurrence among natives of the Pacific Islands. What are you suggesting, Mr. Grant?"

"I'm wondering if that eagle was tattooed on Mikoff's arm after death."

"You have good reasons for your suspicions?"

"I don't know. I was present when the Jap's body was found. Underneath an overcoat thrown across a chair was a case containing tattooing instruments and pigments. They had been very recently used, last night, I would say."

"Well, whether or not we have postmortem tattooing is a matter easily settled. If we examine the tattooing under a strong lens the appearance will be unmistakable. In post-mortem tattooing the needle holes remain open and do not heal as in the case of living skin. If there is any possible doubt, the absence of carbon in the lymphatic glands would settle it."

"Would immersion in water affect it, say the freshness or depth of colouring?"

"Very little. It depends on the nature of the pigments used. There would, perhaps be some fading, but not much. Well, if the matter is urgent let's get it done. Do you wish to see the body?"

"No."

Grant waited in the private office of the pathologist. In five minutes he returned.

"You are right, Mr. Grant," It is postmortem tattooing."

"And no possible doubt?"

"None. But I will take a look at the glands if you require absolute confirmation. But I can assure you I am right."

"If you are satisfied, Doctor," smiled Grant, "so am I. Thank you."

"It's what you expected, eh?"

"Yes, I suppose it was."

"I'll be frank, I would not have looked for it without direction. What I am trying to determine is how he was rendered insensible before he was drowned in the tank. Well, good luck. I think you may need it."

"I can't help feeling you are right Doctor. By the way, I'd be glad if you would inform Mr. Barnard about the tattooing, but put it to him as your own discovery. I don't want him to know I called here. He might think I've gone behind his back, and, well . . . "

Dr. Silver smiled. "Yes, he would. All right, I'll do that."

Grant drove on to his flat. The hunch he had had about Haiki Yuma had turned out to be a winner. The Old Man was going to be very interested. But it was undeniable that it complicated matters like hell.

7

GRANT PARKED HIS car in the courtyard and went up to his flat. He got out a writing block and sat down at his desk. He was going through a routine, setting down the problems, thinking up what line he must follow if Colonel Borlaise gave him no further instructions. Once the Old Man had set an agent on a trail he seldom interfered with him, expecting him to be smart enough to work alone.

What had he established? There were two Herfs, the real and the double. Bearing in mind the professional manner in which Porthy's brief case had been dipped the odds were,

1. That the bogus Herf was a professional dip and had made the snatch at Lydd.
2. Herf himself gave the talk to the crazy society, "Daughters of Liberty," providing a stone-wall alibi for himself.
3. The information both his Department and Scotland Yard had on Herf was inaccurate in vital details.

4. Zoya Alexandrovna had been a willing party to the theft, the decoy, aware that she was working with a substitute Herf.
5. Herf knew, or suspected, he could be identified by the tattooed eagle. Had the eagle any secret meaning?"
6. The Jap, Haiki Yuma, the expert tattooist, was well known to Herf.
7. Herf murdered all three, his double, Zidkov and Yuma to ensure their silence.
8. Herf went to Woolwich to receive the stolen documents from his double. Was Zoya Alexandrovna there, too? Probably not.
9. Why Woolwich?
10. Herf's double needed only the addition of the eagle on his arm for his body to be accepted as Herf's own. The likeness between the two men must be very close. A twin brother, or relative?
11. Herf had not worried about fingerprints being taken of the dead man. Why? Perhaps he felt there was nothing he could do about that and relied on the tattooing and papers in the pocket to establish identity.

12. The Dutch police record was of the double and not Herf.
13. Porthy was either a traitor or a g'damned fool. Perhaps both. But the manner in which he had lost his brief-case suggested that he was not in collusion. There were too many latent snags for safety.
14. If Porthy was innocent, there was a traitor, probably a senior official, at the F.O. they knew nothing about.

Grant studied his fourteen points. Was Herf really a Russian, working for his country? Or was he running true to previous form and playing a lone hand? The leopard does not change its spots. Double-crossing the Russians, even in London, was an exceedingly dangerous and un-profitable game. If Herf had done that it suggested that the theft of Porthy's docu-ments was in the nature of one last big fling before Herf vanished.

It was possible that the Russians would have Herf's finger-prints among their records. In which case the substitution could be discovered, if they had any suspi-cions. The odds were the body now in the path lab of St. Cross Hospital would be accepted as that of Herf, especially coupled with Zidkov's death at the same time and place.

Why had Zidkov got himself involved in such a business? That is, assuming Herf was double-crossing the Russians. Zidkov was the wrong type. Perhaps he had laid himself open to blackmail. Or had been put on to watch Herf. Not very likely. Zidkov was poor stuff.

And the girl, Zoya? She might well be just a stooge, doing what she was ordered to do and not knowing why.

Or was Herf's double the man who had been known as the C.R.O. Ivan Mikoff? No, McLean had seen the eagle on Mikoff's arm at the Ford works. Mikoff was Herf all right.

The double had evidently been using the old house at Woolwich as a hide-out. Why? How long had he been in this country? How long had he been associated with Herf? Many years, it seemed. If so, it explained a great deal which had been so mysterious about Herf in the past.

That was something on which the police could be relied to dig up the information. He would have to talk to Chief Superintendent John Bellamy about it. His own line must be with the more delicate problems, the obstacle of Diplomatic Privilege, the private life of Porthy, his friends and habits. The Russian security men would be working overtime to uncover the truth, assuming Herf was not acting under Embassy orders.

He saw Zoya Alexandrovna as a possible weak link. He must know more about her and Herf's household, his wife and servants. And he had to get the answers quickly.

Grant read over his list of points again, tore off three sheets from the writing block, put the first in his pocket and carried the other two to the grate, where he set flame to them. Impressions left on writing blocks were a nice source of information.

He went into his bedroom and used the scrambler telephone. Impossible to tap a scrambler wire and make any sense of what you heard. Jenny Taylor answered him.

"He's not here at the moment, Ian," she said.

"That's fine. Come and have lunch with me, Jenny. Even beautiful counter espionage agents must eat sometime. I've got a lot to tell you."

"Picking my brains, eh? Stuck for ideas. All right, collect me here in half an hour. If the Old Man comes in I'll tell him. I'll be in the hall, looking like a film actress out of a job."

"If you were a film actress you'd never be out of a job. Be seing you."

Grant rang off. He just had time to see Bellamy at The Yard, if he was available. He called him on the normal phone. Bellamy was there and could see him.

In the bare, bleak room overlooking the river and County Hall the chief superintendent waited for him. Grant told him in a brief, concise statement what he knew, suspected, and wanted done.

"Nice work," commented Bellamy, smiling. "And fast. You'll be interested to learn that the Jap has been identified. He was neck deep in the dope racket. The antique shop was a front. He was also a receiver of stolen goods, the high-class stuff. His real name was Haiki Haisai, an American subject, wanted by the F.B.I. and the French and Dutch police. The original Jap, Haiki Yuma, has disappeared. He was a British subject and had done time for dope smuggling."

"How long has he been masquerading as the original Jap?"

"That we don't know, but not more than two years."

"What do the Continental police want him for?"

"Dope, and receiving."

"Nothing political?"

"No. But they probably wouldn't tell us if there was that angle. All right then, Grant, leave it to me. I'll get busy at once and let you know any results."

"I want as accurate a time schedule as is possible to obtain."

"You shall have it."

"And not a whisper to the Press about the dead man's identity."

"Rely on that."

Grant left Scotland Yard a little uneasy in case he had revealed too much. But he felt that he had to take Bellamy into his confidence if he wanted the answers. Nevertheless, there was always the danger of a leak to the Press from some subordinate with a pal in Fleet Street. However, Bellamy would appreciate the possibility and guard against it . . . he hoped.

Jenny Taylor was in the hall when he arrived. She was dressed in a grey jacket and skirt that fitted her slim figure to perfection. She didn't look like a film actress. She looked like an ordinary, well-bred girl, a brunette, more beautiful than most, with blue eyes and a lovely smile. A girl more unlike the popular idea of a counter espionage agent would have been difficult to imagine.

Grant thought she looked fresh and young and very sweet. That she did the sort of work she did was just as incredible to him as it would have been to the normal citizen. Most of the women he had worked with had been sophisticated to the point of being hard boiled. Which was just as well, because he could forget then that they were women. He didn't have to worry what might happen to them. They knew all the answers and could look after themselves. A few he had liked. With some he had had temporary liaisons, uncomplicated, brought about by the circumstances of their work and simple responsiveness on both sides.

With Jenny it would be different. There could never be any question of an uncomplicated, simple response. There was an integrity in her which would demand more than a pretence of love. She would never be satisfied with second best. The most he could hope for was the affection of comradeship. But, at least, there was truth between them. He could talk to Jenny in a manner which might have been alarming if he had not been so very sure of her discretion. Talking to her was like talking to a fresh and unwearied adjunct of his own brain. He felt that Jenny had faith in him, a simple, direct faith. Well, wasn't that the solid basis for something deeper?

"The Old Man hasn't returned," she said. "But I've got a little more dope on Porthy, and it smells. Where are you taking me?"

"Henri's. We can talk there."

"What a happy thought! I haven't been there for months."

"I'm full of happy thoughts."

"That's more than I am. I have a feeling that we aren't going to get very far in this case, Ian. All hell is due to break at any moment."

He slipped his hand under her arm as he helped her into the car.

"Then let's enjoy the calm before the storm drowns us."

The head waiter found them a table for two, discreetly shielded by a potted palm. Jenny put her handbag on the table, opened it and took out a slim gold cigarette case. She offered it to Grant. When both cigarettes were lighted, she said:

"Porthy was better acquainted with Zoya Alexandrovna than we knew. She visited him at his flat in Mayfair. She could have been his mistress, although we have no definite evidence. The Russians wouldn't have allowed that unless they had something to gain. Porthy has received letters from Russia, too, probably from his friend, Fergus."

"Have we learned anything more about the girl?"

"No. McLean is working on it."

"Well, Porthy will have to be investigated more than somewhat. Why is Bathic keeping him in Paris?"

Jenny shrugged: "Maybe doing his own private investigation before he reports. Gilray has gone over to bring Porthy back, if Bathic will let him go. We have no authority to demand that he should."

"No, but a hell of a lot of pressure can be brought to bear if Bathic proves awkward."

"Why should he?"

"Hushing up the scandal, safeguarding the honour of the F.O. I wouldn't call Bathic one of the world's super intelligences, would you?"

"No. But I would judge him to be an honest man, if narrow."

"I haven't any faith in professional politicians, Jenny. What does the Old Man think about it?"

"Plenty, but he hasn't confided in me."

"He will. Talking to you helps a man to think clearly."

"You flatter me."

"I don't. It's true."

During the meal they talked little. Grant was acutely aware of her seated opposite him, finding a warm pleasure in watching her, admiring her fresh, composed youth, her wide, blue eyes and her resolute mouth which could relax in such a captivating smile.

Once she gave him a long, level look, her eyes measuring him with a new awareness of what he might be thinking. Aware, too, of a small thrill of pleasurable excitement stirring within her.

When coffee was before them, she said: "Now tell me your news."

Grant told her, hiding nothing, summing it up in short, concise sentences which held so much.

"My goodness, Ian!" she exclaimed softly, "this is big trouble!" Obviously Herf couldn't be in two places at the same time, but I'm sure the Old Man doesn't suspect the truth."

"He hasn't my information. He's going on police records, which are wrong. I don't know how, but they are. I'm hoping John Bellamy will sort it out for us."

"Comparison of the two records may yield something. But it's all so urgent, Ian. That's the dreadful snag. I don't understand it. If Herf is double-crossing the Russians, why didn't he go down to Lydd himself, or somewhere close handy? If he isn't playing crooked, why murder three men who helped him? But not the girl. It doesn't make sense."

"How right you are! If Herf is a genuine Russian agent he has already left England. If he is not, then he will be hiding as much from the Russians as from us. If he's still here, he will not be able to get out through air or sea ports. If he went last night, or early this morning before the hue and cry then we've had it. There'll be no hope of recovering those damned documents."

"What do you suppose those documents are that make them so important?"

"Confidential instructions for Bathic alone. He's on a secret mission to the French. Secret diplomacy. You know what a dirty business that can be. International politics! As healthy as a fever-ridden jungle."

"And we are the people who feed the fever, eh?"

"Yes. Why the hell do we do it?"

"You know very well why you do it, Ian."

"You tell me."

"Because you've got the fire of dangerous adventure in your blood. There is a dash of patriotism, too. But it's a poor second."

"You could be right. But why do *you* do it?"

"For the same reason. I like it."

"I find that quite incredible. Tell me,

how did you first get into this dreadful racket?"

"It's not a dreadful racket, Ian. It's a grand, worthwhile, necessary job that only certain types of people can do successfully."

"Gallant British gentleman, but dirty foreign spy. All right, we both like it. Well, how did you start? I've often wondered."

"Colonel Borlaise is my uncle, my mother's brother."

"Well I'll be damned!" exclaimed Grant. "I didn't know."

"We don't advertise it at work."

"He ought to be ashamed of himself."

"Why?"

"Bringing a sweet girl like you into such——"

"He didn't. I badgered him until he did. I have an honours degree in Russian and German. I knew I could be useful in his work."

"You are. But I still think——"

"Forget it, Ian. I wanted the job. I got it. I like it. I'm sticking to it."

"Not for life, I hope."

She shrugged: "Unless somebody bumps me off."

"Don't talk like that," he retorted

sharply. "One day you'll get married. Marriage and our job make ill bedmates. They don't mix."

"Is that why you haven't married?"

"Not entirely. But I wouldn't ask any girl to marry a man who might——"

"Who might be bumped off. If she was the right girl she'd still be glad to marry you."

"Is that what you really think?"

"Yes."

"Good! When we've got this Herf business straightened out, and if we still have employment, I'll give the matter very serious thought. Well, let's get along to the office. I want to dictate a report to you for the Old Man. Then I must get on with the job."

8

IT WAS AN ordinary Yale type lock. Grant took a small, flat case from his pocket, selected a key with a line of stiff nylon thread in place of teeth and inserted it in the lock. The door opened at the first attempt. He closed the door and looked around.

Heavy curtains were drawn over the windows and the place was in comparative darkness. He switched on the light. It was a neat, formal looking room, without character, probably an exact copy of all the other furnished flats in the building. He switched off the light and drew the curtains apart. The autumn sunlight did nothing to enliven the place. This was not a home, just a place in which to sleep.

Grant worked fast, but with skill and trained routine. The writing-desk wasn't even locked. He went through it methodically, examining all the papers. Porthy was a tidy man. Receipted bills were clipped neatly together in date order. Unpaid bills were kept in a manilla folder. There were only three, all a few days old. There was nothing remarkable about any of them.

The stubbs of several cheque books were placed neatly in one corner of a drawer. There was nothing in them either. The counterfoils of two paying-in bank books were with them, together with one half used. Six months ago Porthy had paid in a cheque for £2,000. Since then his payments-in had been of more or less constant sums, his monthly pay cheque, probably.

There were half a dozen letters signed "Win" and written on expensive notepaper bearing an address in Hampstead, a block of flats. Grant glanced through them. "Win" was more than a trifle indiscreet, she was definitely pornographic. Reading the letters, Grant formed the opinion that Porthy had not come up to her expectations. Indeed, her last letter advised him to find a boy friend.

There were other letters, but they held no particular significance for Grant. He found a well thumbed and rather tattered address book which Porthy must have been using since his teens. He traced "Win" at last, "Mrs. Winifredo Lecramberti." Odd name! He had never heard it before. Or had he? At the moment it escaped him if he had.

He went through the book page by page, looking for names he might recognize. Most of them were women's names. He recognized a name here and there, mostly Foreign Office men and women. There was Fergus's address in Moscow, too. Grant put the book in his pocket. Photostat copies could be made and the book returned.

He searched all the usual places where documents might be hidden. When he had finished he thought there was nothing to be found. He opened one of the doors, opening off the lounge and stepped into a bedroom. Here was the same formal, featureless neatness. He began to search.

In the dressing-table drawer he found a large envelope unsealed, bulging with photographs. He glanced them over. They were of the type usually known erroneously as "French," and had been well handled. Some were plainly professional photographs, printed on post cards, either brought from abroad, or bought in Soho. But a number of them were amateur efforts, mainly of one girl, a bold-eyed, well-developed blonde, about thirty years of age. Grant wondered if this could be "Win." He selected four and slipped them into his wallet.

He was about to explore the bed and the mattress when he heard the click of the lounge door lock. He moved swiftly and silently to a position behind the open door, where he could look through the crack. A girl stood there, glancing around, a tall, slim blonde. She had style. It showed in her shoes, her immaculate white gloves, in the way she carried her head and shoulders. When she moved to the curtains and drew them together there was a lithe, almost feline grace in her movements.

Grant ran her face and body through his mind as if it were an identity card in a selector machine. He tried to match her up with someone he knew, but he got no answer. He could not place her. He had never met her or seen her photograph before.

The electric light in the lounge snapped on. She was out of his narrow field of vision, but he guessed that she was at the writing desk.

He slid out, silently. She was seated at

the desk, her back to him. When he was a few feet away he stopped, watching. She had taken out one of the drawers and was feeling in the back of the cavity. Evidently she didn't find what she wanted for she made a small, frustrated noise in her throat and sat up.

Then, as if aware of him, she turned suddenly. Her eyes opened wide in shocked surprise, her lips parted in a soundless gasp and her hand whipped out for the white suede bag on the desk. Grant snatched it away. He knew from the feel and the weight what it contained.

"Who . . . who are you ?" she demanded, springing to her feet, facing him. She had been frightened, but she was rapidly re-gaining her composure, looking at him with eyes narrowed in wary, uncomplimentary speculation. There was just the faintest trace of American accent in her voice, husky, perhaps with emotion.

Grant studied her in those few seconds before he spoke. She had fine, regular, classical features. She was very beautiful in a cold sort of way. But there was something about her which jarred on his nerves, an odd sense of repulsion. It was a curious sensation for a man who was frankly fond of women.

The lead was in his hands. He didn't intend to lose it. He said, not harshly, but with compelling authority: "That's the question I'm asking. Who are you?"

"And if I don't answer?" Grant gave her full marks for nerve.

"I shall call the police."

She stared at him. If she was afraid she didn't show it.

"I don't think you would, but I can't risk it. I am a friend of Morgan Porthy. I have a key to this flat. That's all I'm saying. You can add up and make it what you like."

"I'd rather you made the addition. It would save a lot of time."

She made a little gesture of annoyance.

"Who the devil are you? What are you doing here? Are you a friend of Morgan?"

"Yes."

"I don't believe it."

"I couldn't care less. I want to know why you have come here. And I want to know who you are. You can talk to me. Or you can talk to the police."

It seemed as if he had convinced her. She said, angrily:

"Oh, damn you, very well. Morgan has a photograph of me. I came to get it back."

"What sort of photograph?"

"If you must know, a nude. Do you have to be so personal?"

"It's not here."

"How do you know?"

"I am acquainted with all Morgan's nudes. He has a nice taste in the female form."

"He may not have had it developed yet. It could be still in the camera. I want that photo. I don't trust him with it."

"But you let him take the picture."

"I was crazy . . . and drunk."

"Don't worry, Morgan only shows his nudes to close personal friends."

"That's what I'm afraid of. Where's his camera?"

"He's taken it with him." Grant opened the handbag and took out a small .25 German automatic pistol. The only other things in the bag were some pound notes and loose silver. "This is an odd kind of make-up equipment," he said.

"I am an American."

"Ah, that explains everything. Nevertheless I think you'd do better without teeth."

Grant snapped out the magazine, emptied it, and pushed it back into the butt. He put the bullets in his pocket. "Now, answer my question, who are you?"

"You've got no right to ask. Go on, call the police, damn you."

"Don't bluff. It won't do. I'm not bluffing. Listen, your friend Porthy is in serious trouble. Do you know where he is?"

"No. He phoned to say he was going abroad."

"When?"

"I don't know, Wednesday night, yes. Wednesday. Are you a policeman?"

"No. Come on, what's your name?"

"Lena Boden, damn you."

"Address?"

"Look here, what's this got to do with me? I don't want my mother to know I'm Morgan's friend, or about the . . . the photograph."

"She will not."

"I wish I could trust you."

"You've got no option."

"Oh, very well, Manlock Mansions, number twelve. Now, I'm going. Give me my bag."

Grant gave her the bag. She almost

snatched it from him and walked to the door. She did not look at him again before she went out, leaving the door open.

He went over and closed it. Then he knelt at the desk, feeling in the cavity, wondering what she had been seeking. He found nothing, but he made a mental note to have the desk examined by an expert. There might be some secret pocket which the girl had known about.

But he thought she had spoken the truth. From the discoveries he had made it squared with the possibilities. Porthy was still an adolescent, nasty-minded youth with perverted sex instincts. The girl had had second thoughts about the photograph he had taken of her and wanted it destroyed. She might have felt Porthy wouldn't do that. She was probably right.

Grant could still feel the girl's presence. What, he wondered, was it about her that he found so repulsive? She was, judged by any standards, beautiful of face and form. She had grace and, no doubt, considerable charm if she liked you. It was very odd.

He made a quick finish of the flat. He found nothing to suggest that Morgan Porthy was a traitor. He was about to leave when he saw the key on the floor. For a moment he thought he had dropped the key he had used. When he picked it up he knew it was not his key. The nylon thread was a lighter colour yellow and a little coarser, and his own key was in the case.

It must have been lying on the desk, hidden from view. He had knocked it off when he snatched the white handbag. If he had seen the key first it would have been a very different story. Only crooks and secret service agents possessed such keys.

The gun in her bag should have warned him. But he had known American women who played around who carried those neat little handbag automatics for protection. He had persuaded himself that the girl was another such and she had brought the gun in case Porthy turned up, got rough and refused her demand for the return of her photograph.

Grant stood in the middle of the room, silently cursing himself for a fool, a simple, credulous mug who had been well and truly taken for a ride by an accomplished actress, a woman with nerves of steel and razor-edged wit. Too late now to trail her.

He went over and took up the telephone, dialling Jenny Taylor's official number. She would break it gently to the Old Man and set in motion all that had to be done.

9

JENNY WAS WAITING for him in one of the ground floor offices. She said: "It's all right, Ian. I've reported to the Old Man. He's not too wild about it."

"But I am, Jenny. I've been plain damned stupid. I fell for her like a bucket of lead."

"Is she so beautiful?"

"She is. But there's something about her I find repellant, like a snake. One thing of which I am sure, she's no stranger to Porthy's apartment. The name and address were phoney, of course."

"Yes."

"That desk will have to be taken apart, just in case there is a secret compartment. She was searching for something with the drawer taken out. Better have it done at once, Jenny."

"I've fixed it, but there's not all that hurry now, Ian"

"Why?"

"Porthy is dead."

"Dead? How come?"

"He fell from his bedroom window at the Paris hotel. He was dead when they picked him up. Gilray reported not ten minutes ago."

"Murder or suicide?"

Jenny shrugged. "It looks like suicide, but, of course, it could be murder. He was alone at the time."

"Does the Old Man want to see me?"

"Yes. Mrs. Lecramberti is on our records. She was involved in the Italian political scandals two years ago. If she hadn't slipped out of Italy she would probably have been arrested."

"I'm getting old. My memory must be failing. Now, I suppose I have to work on her?"

"Yes. Maybe you'll like it. She must be very seductive."

"Remind me to slap you sometime. Well, if I have to see the Old Man let's get it over. Anything else come in?"

"If there has, I've not been told. You go up. I have some work to do down here. Drop in as you leave, if I'm not back."

Colonel Borlaise greeted Grant with a curt nod and waved him to a chair.

"All right," he said. "Give me the story."

Grant told him exactly what had happened, Borlaise listened in silence until he had concluded.

"You didn't recognise this woman?"

"No, sir."

Borlaise opened the file on his desk before him. He pushed a glossy print toward Grant. "Is that the woman?"

Grant looked at the photograph, taken at a dinner. He recognized Morgan Porthy. Next to him was the girl, wearing a low-cut evening gown. She was smiling into the camera.

"Yes sir. That is the same woman."

"Zoya Alexandrovna," said Borlaise.

"Good God!" exclaimed Grant.

"Don't let it worry you too much, Grant. You let yourself be fooled. But by and large I feel it might be lucky that you did. She may think she completely fooled you. The point is, was she there on her own private account, or as a Russian agent?"

"The key, sir."

"Yes, I agree. But we don't know how she obtained the key. She is supposed to be nurse-companion to Mrs. Mikoff, Mrs.

Herf, if they are really married. We don't know enough yet about the set-up of that household. If Herf is double-crossing the Russians, Zoya Alexandrovna may be in it, too, with Porthy as her dupe. You are sure she didn't figure in that bundle of nude pictures?"

"I am, sir. But, of course, you can check."

"And cameras?"

"Only one, sir. Empty. There was no undeveloped film. He did his own developing. There was nothing there. I brought four of the nudes away. Maybe we can identify them."

Grant put the four photographs on the desk, together with the address book. Borlaise looked at each photograph in turn, studying them. He put two aside. "Mrs. Vera Klutz," he said. "The other is Mrs. Winifredo Lecramberti. A nice pair, Grant! There's not much we can do with Klutz while her husband is covered by diplomatic privilege, but Lecramberti is vulnerable. She can be deported. Porthy had some peculiar friends for a man in his job."

"A peculiar type altogether, sir."

"Yes. His best friend, Paul Fergus was a homosexual. If he hadn't skipped when he did the police would have had him. I supposed Jenny has told you what has happened to Porthy?"

"Yes, sir."

"We'll know more about it when Gilray gets back. In the meantime I want you to tackle Winifredo Lecramberti. Here's her file. Study it. Then make her reveal all she knows about Porthy, his associates and habits. You might get a line on Zoya Alexandrovna. Take a chance and go to the Hampstead flat. She's still there. Don't telephone first. She's nobody's fool, that woman. So be careful. There's nothing further from Bellamy, or Interpol yet. All right, Grant. Leave the file with Jenny."

As Grant rose to go, he said: "Porthy paid in £2,000 to his bank about six months ago, sir. It's the only big sum I could trace."

"I've checked on that. It was a legacy from an aunt."

Grant took the file into the next room and sat down to learn all about Mrs. Lecramberti, who had no inhibitions about satisfying the photographic urges of the late Morgan Porthy.

She was thirty years of age, born of Swiss-German mother and French father. She had married at eighteen Arnoldi Lecramberti, a minor police official. At nineteen she had deserted him for an Italian artist, son of a wealthy and influential politician. The young man had introduced her in to the vicious circle of high-life society, where every form of vice flourished. She had very soon become the life and soul of the party.

Twice she had been connected with very ugly scandals involving young girls, one of whom had died. High influence had saved her. Possibly as the price she had to pay she became involved in espionage. As a result of her work a Roumanian diplomat shot himself.

There was no record of the actual work she did, but it did not appear from the record to have lasted long. All the while she was carrying on with the vicious circle of friends. When the scandals became too public the bubble burst. She got out of Italy just in time. The government fell and the police stepped in.

Obviously with plenty of money at her disposal, she set up in Paris as a beauty expert. It wasn't long before she had worked herself into good society and become the close friend of politicians.

For some reason, not recorded, she left Paris in a hurry and arrived in London. She set up as a teacher of languages, which she was still supposed to be. The Metropolitan Police had her registered as an alien, with a permit to stay.

An Italian diplomat had introduced her to Porthy at an Embassy party and Porthy had spent the night with her. This had been duly noted and she had been watched. But there was no evidence that she was engaged in espionage. Attached to her record was a list of men known to be on intimate terms with her.

Grant shrugged as he read them. Mrs. Winifredo Lecramberti, he thought, knew how to throw the protective mantle of money and influence around her. Not that it would make any difference in his approach to her. He knew how he had to act. If the Old Man put on the pressure that protective mantle would soon vanish. Public figures were sensitive about their private lives. Usually a carefully guarded hint was sufficient.

Jenny came in as he was about to leave.

"I was coming to look for you," he said. "I have to leave this file with you."

She glanced at the name as he handed her the file.

"Winifredo Lecramberti, eh? So you are going."

"Read it, Jenny. She must have something, that woman. Men eat out of her hand. I'm on my way to mix it with her. Maybe I'll have to bite her hand when she feeds me."

"I have read it, Ian. Why are men such utter fools?"

"That's the way they're made. Woman, the seducer. It frightens me."

Jenny did not smile. She opened the file. "Look at those names. It's quite incredible. We work like slaves. Fools like that are a constant menace to all our good work, and there is nothing we can do about it."

"It's always been the same, Jenny. Think of Mary Ann Clarke. She must have been a headache. Well, wish me luck with the seductive Winifredo. What a stupid name!"

"Good luck, Ian. You'll need it. Be tough. You hold all the aces."

Jenny watched him go. She hated the idea. She hoped he would be ruthless. She thought he would, especially after his slip-up with Zoya Alexandrovna. That was an odd, affair, too! It was out of character. The Russians didn't work that way. She wondered if Finlay and Roberts, working on the desk, would discover anything.

The buzzer sounded. She took up the file and went in. Colonel Borlaise handed her the two photographs.

"Grant brought these from Porthy's flat. Have them filed. That's Klutz, that's Lecramberti. There's a lot more in the flat. We'll have them over. Do you recognize either of those women?"

He handed her the other photographs. Jenny studied them.

"I don't know this one," she said, putting it down on the desk. "But this is Mollie Van Dansen, I think."

"So?" said Borlaise, almost a note of satisfaction in his voice. "We'll have to make sure. A little co-operation from her father would be a great help to us."

Jenny said: "That would be rather dirty, wouldn't it?"

Borlaise leaned towards her, pointing. "Listen, Jenny, I've heard you say that before. There is nothing dirty in this job if it yields the results we want. You don't play with kid gloves and a nice set of rules. It's too serious. Remember that."

"I'm not likely to forget it," she said, smiling. "When am I going to get some field work again?"

"You're too valuable to me here."

"I feel I could be some help to Ian Grant."

"When Grant needs help he'll ask for it."

"I don't think he would ask, not for the sort of help I could give."

"That's what I mean. Don't argue, Jenny."

She looked at his hard eyes and knew it would be futile. No doubt he had it all planned. She took up the file and photographs and went out. She suspected that she might have revealed some of her secret feelings to him.

Colonel Borlaise watched her go. So that was it! Maybe he would have to speak to Grant about it if he saw any developments.

10

GRANT RANG THE bell three times before he got any action. He knew there was someone at home because he could hear bath water running. The running stopped. He heard the click of the lock and the door opened. He recognized her from the photograph.

She had her hair cut in the latest fashion, light tawny hair that glistened like a halo. Her skin had a satin texture and her lips were full and red. She wore a pale blue house coat with a zip down the front. Her eyes were green and they regarded Grant with quick appraisal, summing him up and liking what she saw.

"Madame Lecramberti?" he asked, politely, giving her a smile.

Her voice was low and husky, like a soft caress.

"Yes, I am Madame Lecramberti. Please come in."

Grant walked into a lounge comfortably and expensively furnished in a colour scheme of green, gold and cream.

She said, smiling: "May I get you a drink?"

"No thank you."

She looked at him, her eyes bright, twinkling with good humour, even amusement. Grant wondered if she recognized him.

"You sound like a policeman," she said. "I hope not. You'd make me nervous."

Grant looked at her. He thought it would take a hell of a lot to make Winifredo Lecramberti nervous. What a woman! He was beginning to understand why she was such a success with men. She didn't look hard or evil or treacherous. She looked a damned attractive blonde with laughing lips and seductive eyes. He suspected that the house coat was her only garment. It wasn't going to be easy, but he could play it her way.

"I'm not a policeman," he smiled. "God forbid. I want some information about Morgan Porthy. I am a colleague. I understand you knew him well?"

She was quick.

"*Knew* him?" she exclaimed. Grant felt sure she didn't know what had happened to Porthy.

"Unfortunately, he is dead."

"Dead? When? How?"

"He died in Paris today."

"Was he in trouble?"

"That is why I am here, Madame Lecramberti. If you knew him so very intimately . . . "

"No, no," she protested," you're wrong. I didn't know him all that intimately. He was just a friend."

"Intimately enough to pose in the nude for him. Or wouldn't you consider that particularly intimate?"

She laughed. Her eyes lighted up as if she really was amused.

"Do *you* want to see me in the nude, too?" Her voice was a whisper of invitation. She began to finger the zip fastener, opening it. "I was just going to have my bath."

"Not while I'm on duty," said Grant. "I have to think clearly."

"Too bad, such a big, strong, handsome man! Not like poor Morgan. Sit him by the fire with a bundle of French photos and he'd be happy for hours. That's how he got rid of his urges. I felt sorry for him. He was such a bundle of tangled emotions. I tried to straighten him out, but he was hopeless. I think he missed his friend Paul Fergus."

"Did you know Fergus?"

"No, he told me about him. His kind make me feel a little sick."

"Yes, me too. I want you to tell me all you know about Porthy's foreign friends, men and women."

Grant had been standing by the fireplace. She pointed to the divan. "Let's be comfortable, Mr—— ?"

"Grant."

"No Christian name?"

"Ian. But let's keep this on a business footing. Remember I'm here on duty."

"Too bad! Never mind. Sit down. I won't try to seduce you."

Grant sat down. She sat beside him, as he had known she would. Well, maybe she'd say more that way.

"Do you think you could?" he asked, a mocking smile on his lips.

"I am sure of it, if you'd give me a chance."

"You could be right. Well, how many of Porthy's foreign friends do you know?"

"You're making a mistake, Ian. I didn't know Morgan Porthy all that well. I met him at a diplomatic party. I only saw him half a dozen times. I got very tired of him. He wanted to photograph me. So I let him. Why not? I like men, and I like being photographed. It's very flattering to think they spend hours studying one's picture and letting their imaginations run full."

Grant believed her. She was quite without shame or a shred of morals. She probably did get a big kick and a lot of secret pleasure. He had never met a woman quite like this before. But, oddly enough, she didn't disgust him. Her record showed that she was just plain bad, treacherous, faithless and immoral. Yet she was an amusing woman. He thought a psychiatrist would meet his match in her. Grant found such utter lack of morals fascinating.

"But you knew his friends," he persisted.

"The only ones I knew were a Polish man and an American girl. Morgan was crazy about the girl. The Pole I saw only once, at Morgan's flat. I can't even remember his name."

"The girl's name?"

"Zoya something. Is it important?"

"It could be. What does she look like?"

She gave a very accurate if slightly spiteful description.

"Zoya Alexandrovna," said Grant. "She is supposed to be a Russian."

"She speaks English with an American accent. But she speaks Italian with a German accent. Not very fluently, but very correctly, as if she learned Italian in Austria."

"So you think she is not Russian?"

She shrugged, an elegant lift of the shoulders and movement of her slim hands.

"I wouldn't know. American may mean any race on earth. If she's not, she learned her English in America."

"I take it you don't like her?"

"You take it correctly. There is something unnatural about her."

"Such as?"

"I don't know, and that's honest, Ian. Maybe I don't like women."

"Did Porthy ever photograph her?"

"No, but he tried hard enough. She wouldn't take her clothes off. Perhaps that's what I thought odd about her."

She laughed, a merry ripple of genuine mirth. Grant found himself wondering if she was really as vile as her record suggested. He checked the thought.

"How many people do you know at the Russian Embassy?" he demanded.

"Only one, a public relations man, or something."

"Mikoff?"

"Yes."

"How well do you know him?"

"I met him at a diplomatic party, too, through the Pole. He came here offering me a job at the Embassy. But I didn't fall for that one. I've had enough trouble through fiddling in politics. One thing I have learned, you can't trust Russians. Which reminds me, he came once to Porthy's flat while I was there."

"Alone?"

"No. He came with the Pole and the Zoya girl. They were all dressed up, going somewhere with Porthy. I was thrown out. That was the last time I saw Porthy. I wrote and told him what I thought of him."

"You advised him to find a boy-friend."

Her eyes narrowed and for the first time Grant observed some flicker of unease.

"So the beast kept my letters! Well, I hope you enjoyed reading them."

"I found them most educational."

She laughed, all the unease apparently gone.

"Where are they now?"

"In the files."

She leaned forward, looking into his eyes questioningly.

"Is this blackmail?"

"No."

"What then?"

"I want the truth about Mikoff."

"You've had it."

"Listen, Winifredo, I'd hate to threaten anyone so beautiful and seductive as you, but this is serious business."

"What would you threaten?"

"Deportation."

He could see she was thinking hard about that.

"I thought you were such a nice man, too! The type I fall hard for. We could have been such good friends."

"We still can be. What have you to hide?"

She looked at him, doubtfully, as if trying to come to a decision. She said: "If you know my history you will know that I've had plenty of trouble with politics. I don't want any more. I'm nicely settled here. I'm happy for the first time in my life. I've been a bastard. I still am. But I'm steering clear of political intrigue. That's a stupid game for any woman."

"You don't have to be involved in politics, Winifredo," he said gently. "All I'm asking you to tell me is how and when you met Mikoff, if that's his real name, and what he is really doing in this country."

"How much do you know about him?"

Grant shook his head.

"I can't tell you that, as you must know, with all your experience. But I can check my information against anything you tell me. And will you believe me when I say that your confidence will not be betrayed. We still have some code of honour and one of the rules is not to betray an informant. It pays dividends."

He had convinced her. It gave him a small thrill of satisfaction that he could force his will on such a woman.

"All right," she said. "But do let us have that drink, Ian. And a smoke."

"Very well. Whisky for me, if you have it." He slipped out his case and offered her a cigarette. "I'll pour the drinks, shall I?"

"Afraid I shall dope you?" she retorted

laughing. "In the cabinet, over there. A gin and lime for me. Make it man sized."

Grant poured the drinks. He gave her her glass and she raised it, smiling at him.

"Good luck, Ian," she said. "I wonder if I'm going to like knowing you."

"Why not?"

She shrugged, just a little wearily.

"I've known so many men. Not one cared a damn about me really. I ought to play coy and hard to get. But I'd hate it. I'm a lonely woman, if you could believe that."

What comes next? thought Grant. Aloud he said: "You haven't met the right sort of men. Now tell me about Mikoff."

"I don't know how much you have found out about him, but let me say at once, he's smart, slick and dangerous."

"You don't have to tell me that," smiled Grant. "Go on."

"He may be a Russian, he may not, I don't know. He speaks the language like a native. So he does Polish and German. His English has a heavy accent, but I can't place it. I met him first in Rome, three years ago. He wasn't on the Embassy staff or in the diplomatic game, as far as I know.

He was called Heffle then and was supposed to be an Austrian.

"If you have my history, you will know that I was tied up with scandals in Rome. Those wild parties were nobody's business. Things went on there that even I couldn't improve upon. Heffle was the drug supplier. I was his agent. Once I'd begun to work for him he had me, body and soul. I couldn't have broken from him if I'd wanted to. He was well in with the police. A word from him and I'd have gone inside for life. You must believe me, Ian."

"I do. I know the pattern."

"I wouldn't be so stupid as to lie to you when you must know so much."

"Fine," said Grant. "Go on. You were scared of the man, eh?"

"I was. I wanted to quit. But he knew it. I tried to make a break after a dreadful night when one of those wild parties got out of hand. A fifteen year old girl died. Another was only just saved. Heffle warned me that I'd be the Number One suspect and it was futile to hope to escape him. I was taken and grilled for hours by the police before Heffle intervened secretly and I was released. But I had to pay for it."

She paused, taking a long pull at her drink. He observed that her fingers were quivering. If it wasn't genuine it was a damned smart imitation.

"He asked his price. What was it?"

"He told me I had to get intimate with a man who was first secretary at one of the Balkan Embassies. I was introduced to him at a political party and I worked on him. He was quite young and very handsome. I think he became really fond of me. Heffle gave me a drug to put in his drinks while I had him in my apartment. I hated it, but I had to do it. Heffle robbed him of his keys and papers. He came back about dawn and put the keys and papers back. The young man never knew it had happened. The next thing I heard was that he had shot himself."

"He was a Roumanian?"

"Yes."

"Did you ever learn what happened?"

"The Embassy secret safe was robbed of important documents. There were only two keys, one with the Ambassador, the other with him."

"How did you learn that? Surely it was kept secret."

"Oh, it was. I learned it from another member of the staff with whom I was friendly."

Grant was thinking Embassy staffs could be a menace to their countries. He was remembering what had happened in Turkey and Greece at the British Embassies. It was all part of the routine, of course. The British probably had their agents in every foreign Embassy in the world, or in close touch with the staffs. So did every major power.

"Were you scared lest you should be involved?" he asked.

"I was. I went in terror of my life. I felt as he had spent that night with me I was bound to be suspected and someone would slip a knife into my back when I wasn't looking."

"Lucky it didn't happen. What next?"

"The newspapers began to publish more than a hint of the wild parties and the scandals. The father of the girl who died was quite a prominent man, a banker. He was out for revenge. The papers published names, of politicians and men in public life, and even a photograph of a party in progress. It all happened very fast. There were actions brought in the Courts against the newspapers, but before they could be heard the government had fallen, and the police were active. I fled, secretly, one night, telling no one. I had made a lot of money and I had banked it in Switzerland against just such an emergency. I had a small fortune in jewels, too. I got clean away and reached Paris the next day. I had a friend there. He hid me until I could be sure I was safe."

"Safe ? From whom, Heffle or the Italian police ?"

"Both. But chiefly Heffle. I wasn't very much worried about the Italians. I knew enough to ensure either protection or to turn police witness. In any case, I had never lost my Swiss nationality. I couldn't be extradited from France."

"You had it all worked out very well," smiled Grant. "Clever of you. You set up business as a beauty specialist in Paris, I believe."

She shot him a quick glance and her lips softened in a smile.

"You've got it all worked out, too, haven't you ?"

"Most of it."

"Then you'll know I'm telling you the truth."

"I do. I never doubted you, Win."

She put out her hand and patted his lips, softly, drawing the tips of her fingers over his mouth.

"How nicely you lie, Ian, darling. You are so sweet. I could love you. Yes, I set up as a beauty specialist. I bought an existing business from a smart society woman who was near bankruptcy. I paid her a big price. I had the money. Believe it or not, I let her go on acting as proprietress while I became her assistant. That way I got to know a lot of women, and through them their husbands. I had a wonderful time."

"Then the bubble burst. Why?"

"Don't you know?"

"Maybe, but you tell me."

"You still don't trust me, do you?"

"Not yet. But I shall."

"Yes, you will. I feel it in my heart that we are going to be good friends. You know what a bad woman I've been. I don't have to pretend to you. I like it that way."

"Why did you leave Paris in such a hell of a hurry?"

"Because I saw Heffle again, in Paris. He

pretended he didn't know me. But I knew he was up to something. I was right."

"Tell me."

"I was in a restaurant. It was very crowded. I had to sit at a table for six. I was alone, taking a quick meal before I returned to the beauty parlour. Heffle came in. There was only one spare seat, on my table at the other end. He stared at me. I was quite shocked, and frightened. I finished my meal quickly and left. He followed, although he hadn't even given his order to the waiter. I managed to shake him off by going in the front entrance of a building I knew and walking quickly through the back, in another street. I went straight to an agent, put my business up for sale and left the same night for London. I had friends here."

"You have friends everywhere," smiled Grant. "Go on."

"I had to have some reasonable excuse to settle in this country without being worried by the police. So one of my friends suggested I became a teacher in a School of Languages in which he had an interest."

"Have you ever taught?"

"Yes, I still do for special pupils, diplomats mainly. I am quite a linguist, Ian. I learn languages very easily."

"Are you quite sure it was Heffle you saw in Paris?"

"Oh, yes, quite sure."

"It could have been a double. We all have doubles, you know. They crop up in the most remarkable manner, too."

"But I was sitting only a yard or so from him. It was Heffle, all right. My God, I wouldn't make a mistake about that man. Besides, I recognized the small scar on his chin. And why should a stranger follow me?"

Grant laughed. "Several reasons. He thought you were a very lovely woman and wanted to get acquainted. Or he saw you look scared and wondered what it was all about. So he followed."

"No," she said, "it was Heffle. Damn it, Ian, would I be mistaken in a man who had lived with me and whom I had come to fear and hate? No, of course not."

"All right, I agree. I was just making sure. Did Heffle have any tattoo marks on his body?"

"Yes, a small eagle on his right forearm."

"Did he ever tell you how he came to be tattooed?"

"No, but I saw the same small eagle on the arm of a Pole. That was in Paris. He was leading a Polish trade mission. He told me that it was the sign of a brotherhood, or society. I was not very interested. I think it's quite stupid to be tattooed."

"What was the Pole's name?"

"Oh, let me think. I remember, Eric Siloffski. His mother, he said, was English. He was a very nice man."

"It was an identical eagle to the one on Heffle's arm?"

"Yes, it was. I recognized it at once."

"Did you tell him about Heffle."

"No, I did not. I was trying to forget I'd ever met him."

"Well, you came to London. How did you meet Heffle again?"

"I told you, at a party, through the Pole."

"Whose name you can't remember."

She leaned towards him and put her hand on his thigh. He let it stay.

"Listen, Ian, I am telling you the truth. I do not remember the man's name. I may not even have heard it, although I suppose I must have done sometime. If it's important, I could find out."

"It may be. Was he a diplomat?"

"Yes, I think so, a commercial agent, or something. Not one of the big shots, anyway."

"So Heffle came here, not I presume at your invitation."

"Certainly not. He rang the bell and I found him standing there on the mat. He pushed past me and walked in."

"What did he want?"

"To work for him again in drugs and seducing men."

"What was your reaction?"

"At first I was very frightened. But I knew I had only to ring up one of my friends and I would be safe. I refused. After that I didn't feel scared anymore."

"How did he take it?"

"Just laughed. He said he had a way of taming me. But he didn't explain. He shrugged and left. It was all over in fifteen minutes."

"Did he give you any idea how he was operating in the drug traffic?"

"He said he had the perfect set-up working. He had a couple of men at the docks and a Japanese already in the trade. I didn't listen to half of what he said. I had made up my mind that I'd see him in hell before I'd let him master me again. Besides, I hate the drug traffic. I've seen how it works. Once I used to think it was a wonderful way of making money. I don't now."

"And he has not troubled you since?"

"No. I've been waiting for trouble, but it hasn't come."

"You have no idea how he came to be employed by the Russians as their C.R.O."

"None whatever. I could ask among my friends. But you never get the truth about the Russians. They spend their lives watching each other and never talk about anything that really matters."

"You could try and find out," Grant said.

"If you really want it."

"I do. You could be a great help to me, with all your contacts."

"I'd love to help you, darling. But if it means . . ."

"It would not. Just keep your eyes and ears open and ask a clever question in and out, that's all."

"If it's no more than that, then I'm your woman. At least it will make you come to me again."

"That's grand! Now I must be on my way."

"Do you have to be in such a hurry?"

"I'm afraid so."

She rose beside him and stepped in close against him. Her lips were like a burning cushion against his own. When he put his arm about her shoulder he found it was bare. He had been right. The house coat was her only garment and she had let it slide to the floor.

11

WHAT A WOMAN! What a hell of a woman! Grant was thinking as he slid into the driving seat. If it hadn't been for Jenny he knew quite well he would have yielded. The desire she had created in him was near overmastering. Only by a very definite effort of will had he finally resisted her incredible appeal.

He hoped he hadn't offended her. He thought not. She would try again when she had some information she could give him. He wondered just how far he could trust her. The threat of deportation had shaken her, so, maybe, she wouldn't try too much to deceive him.

Grant told Jenny the whole story, all but the final incident. He didn't think it was necessary for her to know that.

"There is nothing in our records about any chin scar," Jenny said. "Did you notice it when you viewed the body?"

"No. It must be very small."

"Or wasn't there."

"We'd better check with Dr. Silver. It's an important detail. Get him on the phone now. If he's not there his registrar will do."

Jenny called St. Cross Hospital. Dr. Silver was there.

"Yes," he agreed, "there is a small scar, crescent shaped on his chin. You probably missed it because of the stubble."

"Can you say how old it is?" asked Grant.

"No. When once a scar has become firm and white there is no data of a medical nature which will enable us to say when the wound producing it was inflicted. It could be twelve months or twelve years."

"So it's not a new scar?"

"That depends on what you mean by new. It is clearly not less than, say, two months old. There are such wide variations in the time. This particular scar is the result of a clean, incised wound. It would have formed much more rapidly than a larger ragged wound."

"Could it have been made by a surgeon?"

"It could have been. But what would be the point? There is no operation which would necessitate that kind of incision. If I had to hazard a guess I would say the scar is several years old. It looks as if it could have been made by the hollow end of a sharp-edged, rounded tube. But that's no more than a guess. Why do you want to know?"

"For the same reason as I wanted to know about the tattooing, Doctor. I am much obliged to you and apologize for troubling you. Good-bye."

Grant replaced the instrument on its cradle. Jenny put down the extension on which she had been listening.

"So that's that," she said. "Now we know that both men had similar scars on their chins. A most incredible coincidence."

"It does happen."

"I know. In this case, in view of the tattooing, post-mortem, it stands out a mile that one or the other had the scar artificially produced."

"Then why not the tattooing, too?"

"Because the tattooing was always hidden by the coat sleeve. It wasn't necessary for the double to have it."

"So which one scared the pants off Winifredo Lecramberti?"

"In the Paris restaurant?"

"Yes."

"Herf's double."

"Because he didn't appear to recognize her?"

"Yes. Herf had been her master, body and soul, on her own confession, for what that may be worth."

"I believed her," declared Grant. "That, at least, I think was true."

"Very well. He would have felt that he still had power over her. There was no point in pretending he didn't know her unless there was some other person present from whom he wished to conceal their relationship."

"That, I feel we can assume, is most improbable."

"I agree. Herf would not have let her slip away from him as easily as she did. I think the meeting was purely accidental. The man was intrigued by her show of fear. He guessed she had mistaken him for Herf and wanted to know what it was all about. Which suggests to me that the two men kept their private lives apart and only worked together professionally. Otherwise the double would have known her."

"It doesn't get us anywhere, Jenny."

"Well, who knows? The double was in Paris at that time. When he is identified we might be able to check back and discover what he was doing there. According to our records Herf was still in Rome."

"Those records are unreliable. The two men have been confused. That, doubtless, was the whole idea of their association. What have we on Eric Siloffski?"

Jenny consulted a card index, one of dozens in steel cases lining the walls.

"Nothing," she said.

"It may not be his name. Perhaps the Old Man will know. Where is he?"

"Gone to Paris at Sir George Bathic's urgent request."

"Alone?"

"Yes. He expects to be back tonight"

"Not so good," declared Grant. "I think this really is serious. Is there any further information from the C.I.D.?"

"No, not yet. What are you going to do next, Ian?"

"Take a good look at the inside of Herf's residence. It has to be done."

"Tonight?"

"Yes."

Jenny nodded. "That's what I anticipated. Is it really necessary? Is it likely that he would keep anything of great importance in his house?"

"No, maybe not. But if he's still in this country he must be hiding somewhere."

"And if he is there, what then?"

"He's not covered by Diplomatic Privilege. I shall call John Bellamy and have him knocked off."

Jenny looked worried. "What chance would we have then of recovering the stolen documents?"

"If the documents are still in this country and Herf is arrested, charged with murder, the odds are they will stay here. With time their danger may cease. Plainly they are dangerous now. But it seems to me that if we can tide over the next week, say, without them being handed on, then we stop the threatened explosion. Do you agree?"

"I don't know. We are not aware of the contents. That's the snag. They could always be a potential source of danger."

Grant smiled: "We can cope with potential danger, Jenny. It's the immediate and urgent danger which may beat us. I must take a look into that house."

Jenny knew that he had made up his mind. She said: "What if the police are not ready to make a murder charge stick. As I see it they have a mass of probabilities and a great deal of suspicion, but no evidence that the Director of Public Prosecutions would consider safe to bring into Court on a murder charge, especially against a Russian embassy official. The newspaper boys all over the world would go to town on it with flaming headlines. Too bad if a jury found him innocent."

"I've thought of that. I'll have to consult Bellamy before I suggest an arrest."

"Which may reveal your intention to burgle Herf's house. The police will not like that very much, Ian."

Grant laughed. "Oh, come off it Jenny," he protested. "I'm not that dumb."

"I'm just a little anxious for your safety. You take such terrible risks, sometimes when you don't have to."

"Only just a little anxious?" asked Grant, smiling but knowing that the answer was important to him.

She looked at him, quickly, and away, seeing the expression in his eyes.

"Would you have me more anxious?"

"No," said Grant, definitely, almost violently. "It might make me too cautious. When a man gets that way he's heading for disaster. You know that, Jenny. I don't have to tell you. Bill Lavers died because he had a wife too anxious about him. He was thinking of her and not his job. He was just the split second too slow because his mind was troubled."

"Poor Bill! It wasn't only his wife, Ian. His nerve was going anyway. If there had been someone else to send the Old Man would not have risked him. I'd like to come with you if you go tonight."

"Breaking-in?"

"Yes."

Grant shook his head. "No, Jenny, my dear. It's a one-man job."

"I'd be in the way?"

"I didn't say that."

"You thought it."

Grant stared at her. Then, moved by a sudden impulse, he took her in his arms and held her tightly. He put a hand under her chin, tilting up her face.

"You've asked for it," he said. "If I had some safe job I should have asked you to marry me long ago. You know I can't ask you. You know why."

Jenny's eyes were bright as she looked up at him.

"I always think it is wise for a man to marry a woman who understands the difficulties of his profession," she said. Better still if she is in it herself."

"My God, Jenny, my love, you make it hard."

"I thought I was making it easy, Ian, darling."

"This is pure madness," protested Grant, and kissed her with unrestrained passion, holding her tightly, forgetting everything in the wonder of the moment. Her arms were about his neck, warm and soft and possessive.

The loud, insistent ringing of the telephone brought them back to reality. For those few golden moments they had forgotten it.

12

THE ESSENCE OF disguise is simplicity. There must be no wigs or false beards to come unstuck at a critical moment, no cumbersome clothes to hamper the wearer in an emergency. Grant was a master in the art of disguise.

When he left the offices of the Industrial and Nature Films he was typical of the poorer class night workers of the West End. His face was the colour of old leather. His finely-cut nostrils were widened and coarsened. A large mole, composed of carpenter's glue and grated leather with a few ugly black hairs added, adorned his left cheek just under his eye, drawing down the lower lid. His hair was a dirty grey and his finger-nails jet black. With his height and weight he looked tough without being too sinister. He looked like a labourer on some sort of night maintenance work, a stoker or oiler.

To help him further the fog which had descended soon after nightfall was thickening.

Grant had deliberately shut all thoughts of Jenny from his mind. This complete mental detachment was something he had achieved only after years of practice. As he walked slowly along Lyttelton Road he was willing himself into the identity he had assumed with his disguise. He was Joseph Brown, the out-of-work stoker, whose National Insurance card, Trade Union card and greasy, tattered Income Tax form he carried in his pocket. If he was searched there was nothing to identify him with Ian Grant. Even his shirt and underclothes were stained, old, and dirty with grease and ash. His socks were thick wool, holed at the toes. His boots were cracking with heat, oil and ash.

The fog was thickening rapidly and he quickened his pace. It would be just too bad if he broke into the wrong house. He came to the road he was seeking and turned in, walking slowly again, counting the gates. This was it, a large, detached house with a surrounding garden and high hedge.

Silently, no more than a dark shadow in the fog, he eased open the gate and walked into the garden. No lights were visible anywhere. He circled the house before he used a slim bladed knife to open a rear window. When he flashed a guarded torch beam it revealed the kitchen.

It was warm, with a lingering smell of cooking in the air. Grant moved across the kitchen to the door. Opening it, cautiously, he listened. The house was silent. He moved into a corridor and found the side door. He turned the key and slid the bolt, making sure of his escape if he found trouble.

The hall was large and square with rooms on either side. Neither door was locked. He began to feel that he was wasting his time. Herf wouldn't be content to lay up in a house so carelessly guarded and vulnerable.

He opened the door to his left. The bright beam of his torch shone on curtains of heavy velvet drawn across windows from floor to ceiling. He closed the door and switched on the lights. The room was furnished, rather barely, as a lounge. Dying embers in the grate showed red points of flame here and there. The faint odour of tobacco still lingered. The room had been used very recently.

It was unlikely that anything of importance would be hidden in such a place. He gave it a quick run over, found nothing and switched off the lights as he stepped into the hall. He tried the other door.

This room was much more promising. It suggested a library-cum-office. Two walls were lined with glass-fronted book-shelves, filled with cheap editions of famous British and American writers. A complete but very aged set of encyclopaedias were mixed with an odd assortment of junk. But in one section were books in German and Russian of a political and scientific nature which appeared to have been well used. Grant thought that, except for these latter books, the library had been taken over from the previous owner as it stood.

He turned his attention to the big desk, which looked as if it were of Continental manufacture, and expensive. It was locked. He brought out his neat little set of tools and went to work. He opened the central drawer without difficulty. It contained only writing paper, envelopes, clips, tags and other odds and ends.

The drawers in the twin pedestals were not so easy. It took him ten minutes of patient manipulation to discover how they were operated. There was an ingenious device and an arrangement of steel rods in the back of the desk which locked them. He had not met anything quite like it before and he discovered the secret more or less by accident.

Before he set himself to work methodically through the desk he went across the room and unfastened the french windows. He emptied each drawer, examining papers, letters and anything he found. Most of them were either in code or in some language he did not know. Those papers which he was able to read were all in German and appeared to be business correspondence concerning old books and manuscripts. The dates ranged over a considerable number of years and none bore either the name of Mikoff or Herf.

It was in the second drawer of the right-hand pedestal that Grant discovered an assortment of passports in different names and issued by several European countries. All bore a man's photograph, and all were vaguely similar to the man he had known as Ivan Mikoff. The main differences lay in beards and moustaches. In the same drawer was a small notebook with shiny black covers. It contained pages of signs and figures which meant absolutely nothing to him. Nevertheless he thought it might be important, so he slid it into his pocket.

He was bending below the level of the desk to open the last drawer when he was aware of a draught of cold air. He leaned lower and peered out between the pedestals. He saw the curtains parted and a pair of feet shod with black shoes.

He felt the sudden thrill of excitement in his blood as very slowly he straightened up. He had guessed correctly. The man who stood just inside the windows had the face of the corpse he had seen at Woolwich mortuary, even, he observed, to the chin scar. This then was the notorious Peter Herf.

Herf was staring at him in mild astonishment. Grant observed that his right hand was in his overcoat pocket, doubtless with his finger on the trigger of a pistol.

"Well," said Herf at last, "this is what I think the English call a fair cop." His voice was harsh, foreign, but without emotion. He was regarding him now with cold interest.

"Yus, guv, a fair cop," replied Grant

with a whining, Cockney accent. "I ain't took nothink."

"What in particular were you seeking?" Herf was moving towards him. Grant stood up and moved out from behind the desk. He put on a cringing expression, as if he accepted his fate.

"Anyfink," he said. "I ain't particular."

"You say you've taken nothing?"

"That's right, guv. I ain't found anyfink good worth taking yet."

"So you opened the desk! Did you have much trouble with it?"

"Some, not much. Somethink went click and then the drawers was easy."

Herf was close to him now. Grant eyed him warily, shrinking away. Herf nodded towards the desk.

"Show me," he demanded.

"Grant was turning when Herf's hand flicked out like the dart of a snake's tongue. Long muscular fingers encircled Grant's throat, squeezing in a stranglehold. For a couple of desperate seconds Grant was actually held on his feet by those murderous fingers. He saw the cold, pitiless light of the killer in the other's eyes. There was no anger. Herf might have been squeezing some inanimate object instead of a man's neck for all the emotion he displayed.

Grant got his back against the desk and heaved himself inwards against Herf. At the same instant he drove his right hand into Herf's Adam's apple, striking not with his fist but with the index and middle fingers held rigidly in a V. He landed with deadly accuracy.

Herf let go his strangle hold, choking. Grant stood back and lashed with his booted foot at Herf's knee. As Herf's head came forward, doubled over with the agony, Grant upper-cut him in a perfect knock-out, dropping him to the floor beside the desk.

Grant went down on one knee and began to search him. He found the automatic pistol and transferred it to his own pocket. He was sliding his hand into the inside jacket pocket when the door opened suddenly, without sound. Grant looked up. Zoya Alexandrovna stood there in the open doorway, a Luger pistol pointing straight at him. She wore a heavy woollen dressing gown of red wool and soft leather bedroom slippers of the same colour.

She didn't look scared. She looked calm and determined.

"Get up," she ordered. "Raise your hands."

Grant obeyed slowly, not because he had any thought to refuse, but to gain that extra second of thinking time. He was masking Herf's head. He guessed she could not see his face.

"Stand over there," she ordered. "Keep your hands up."

Grant was watching her. He saw her eyes flicker to Herf, who lay groaning, showing definite signs of returning consciousness. He saw the sudden expression of incredulity flame in her eyes. He heard her whisper, in Russian: "The fool! Why has he come back?"

In that moment Grant jumped. The Luger exploded as he struck down her wrist, but the bullet ploughed harmlessly into the carpet. He stepped in close, wrenched the pistol from her hand and pushed her against the desk.

"Now, keep quiet," he snarled, "or I'll do yer."

She looked at him as if she had never seen him before. She said: "Get out."

Grant heard feet hurrying down the stairs. He had a brief vision of another woman at the door as he went across the room in a rush, parting the curtains before he dived into the garden. The fog enveloped him like a protecting blanket as he made across the garden to the gate.

At the corner of the road he had observed the telephone kiosk. He went in and dialled Bellamy's number.

13

GRANT WAS MOVING up the road on the other side when he was aware that there was someone ahead of him. He halted, listening into the dense fog, trying to locate the other. Whoever it was had stopped opposite Herf's house. He began to edge forward, silently, his hands held in half hooks before him, ready to stifle any cry.

He was within a yard of the other before he saw the shadowy movement as the person turned towards him. His hands shot out, one smacked hard over a nose and mouth and the other laid flat between shoulder blades. In that second of impact he realized it was a woman. He eased the stifling hand a little and whispered:

"Jenny?"

He felt her lips moving under his palm and lifted his hand.

"Ian, you're hurting me," she whispered.

He put his arm about her shoulder and whispered close to her ear:

"Jenny, darling, this is plain lunacy. Why have you come?"

"I was worried about you. What's happened?"

He told her, whispering, listening for any sounds coming from the house opposite.

"Zoya Alexandrovna is Russian," he said. "She thinks in Russian. When you surprise a person he is apt to speak in his native language, unless he has been very well trained. Zoya plainly thought Herf had left the country."

"But why then has he come back? It was a tremendous risk if he is double-crossing the Russians."

"I don't know. It puzzles me, too. He has something left unfinished."

They heard the car coming up the road, fog lights flaring as it stopped. A car door slammed. A man's voice said: "This is it, Serg."

"Police," whispered Grant in her ear. "They've been mighty quick."

"Bellamy must have sent out a call to the local station."

"More likely to be a prowl car who happened to be close handy. All the same, I wouldn't have thought Bellamy would have used them. It's not a job for the uniformed police. I'm going over and take a look."

"I'm coming with you." Jenny slipped her hand under his arm as if she were afraid of losing him. "We can't be seen in this pea souper."

Crossing the road lower down they eased up towards the house. Presently they heard footsteps and the gate creaked. A shadowy form moved in the misty yellow haze from the headlights. The car door opened and a voice began speaking into the microphone somewhat muffled, but loud enough for them to hear.

"It's murder all right, sir. Looks like she was strangled. Yes, it's Mrs. Mikoff. There's a girl here and an old man, a servant. No, sir, no one else. Yes, we've searched. The fog? It's thick and getting worse. Very good, sir."

The car door closed with a metallic snap. The shadow moved through the misty glow and the garden gate clicked again.

"So what?" Grant's voice was a dry whisper in her ear.

"Mrs. Herf's been strangled. Did you see her?"

"A woman came down the stairs. I saw her for a fleeting second as I beat it through the french windows. If that was Mrs. Herf she was very much alive. How long had you been here when I found you?"

"About five or six minutes. Not more."

"Did you hear anyone come out of the house?"

"No."

In his disguise as a labourer Grant had no watch. He asked Jenny the time.

"That makes it about twenty-five minutes ago I phoned Bellamy. Either the girl or Herf killed her. Somebody telephoned the police. These cops are nothing to do with Bellamy."

"If she was strangled," said Jenny, "it must have been Herf."

"But why?"

"Because she saw him and knew then that he was alive. Herf couldn't trust her not to betray him."

"But he trusted the girl."

"Yes. She must have lied to the police, and probably to the servant. Herf has escaped, unless there's some secret hiding place in the house the police missed. How bad was he when you beat it?"

"He'd have been fully conscious in a minute or so. He's big and tough. He could have done it all right. Stay here, Jenny. Watch and listen. I must phone Bellamy again."

Jenny waited in the fog, listening. It was an eerie business and she didn't like it. What had happened seemed obvious to her. Herf had recovered consciousness, found his wife there and realized that she would inform the Russians. If the Old Man's information was correct, Mrs. Herf was the sister of a high-up in the Communist party. How Herf had come to marry her was just another of the mysteries surrounding the man. He had killed his wife, taking the golden opportunity afforded by Ian's break-in. The police could be expected to put her death down to the burglar. Herf had probably completed the job which had made him venture home under cover of the fog and vanished again. Zoya Alexandrovna would have telephoned the police and probably the Russian Embassy to keep herself in the clear. Whoever the girl might be she was playing an exceedingly dangerous game. She was likely to be Herf's mistress and together they had planned a coup before they fled. Something had gone wrong with their plans and Herf was out on a limb.

Jenny heard the car turn the corner and come slowly up the road. She flattened herself against the privet hedge of the house next door and waited, holding her breath.

A man was walking on the pavement. He passed within a yard of her. At Herf's gate he stopped. She heard him say: "Here we are."

The car doors closed and several shadows moved through the yellow haze of lights. A voice said: "How did this crew get here first?"

If anyone ventured an answer Jenny did not hear it. These, she supposed, were plain clothes men sent by Chief Superintendent Bellamy.

Grant was at her side before she realized he had returned.

"Phew," she whispered, "you startled me! Well, what did Bellamy say?"

"He's going to try and get through himself. He's contacted a patrol car out on a job for him in this area. They've arrived haven't they?"

"Yes. But they're wasting their time. Herf will have escaped."

"It will depend on what made him come back. But I don't think Zoya Alexandrovna would have contacted the police if there was any danger of Herf being found on the premises. There's no rear entrance to these houses, but it would be easy enough to get over the fence of the garden backing on to this one and escape into the next road. Bellamy says he's just received a report from Holland which is very interesting, and they've developed fingerprints of Haiki the Jap, Zidkov and another in the riverside house at Woolwich, all on the table. The Jap could have visited in the capacity of owner, of course, but it's more likely he left his dabs when he was tattooing the eagle on the dead man's arm. So it looks as if Zidkov was working with Herf."

"And Herf murdered him to keep his mouth shut."

"Yes, like the Jap."

"What about the bullets you took from the girl's gun?"

"A probable identification with the finger-prints unidentified at Woolwich. My guess is Herf loaded the gun. I wish I'd confiscated it. There would have been prints on the magazine, unless it was too oily for any clear impressions."

"There ought to be enough in this house to check with," said Jenny. She put her hand on Grant's arm in warning pressure. "Another car coming."

The car came up the road, passed the house, reversed, and came back, parking behind the second police car. Jenny and Grant stood rigidly still. Two men got out and stood by the car. They spoke softly together before they opened the gate and moved in.

"Russians," whispered Jenny.

"Could you hear what they were saying?"

"Only a word or two. They were debating the wisdom of entering while the police were there; I think."

"Zoya Alexandrovna is in for some tough grilling, I guess. I feel we can be sure Herf is double-crossing the Embassy. That pair will be a couple of security men. They'll be just as anxious as we are to nobble Herf, if they know he is still alive. It could very well be that they do not."

"Do you know if anyone from the Embassy has identified the dead man as Mikoff?"

"Yes, one of the secretaries. But I'm thinking they will take another look."

"But if Herf was working without their knowledge they won't know anything about the stolen documents. That's why Herf alibied himself by talking to that crack brained society."

"I don't know. Their security system is very good. They don't trust anybody. But I'm inclined to think Herf outwitted them. That's why he had to murder his wife. I'm wondering what we ought to do now. I can't see we gain anything by staying here."

"Except to get caught by the police. Let's go."

"How did you get here?"

"By car. I parked it at East Finchley station."

"So did I. Come on, let's go. You can leave your car to be collected in the morning. The sooner I'm out of these filthy clothes the cleaner I'll feel."

"Is Bellamy expecting you to stay?"

"No, he told me to go home and leave it to him."

"Well, that's good advice. So, come on, if we can find our way in this fog. It's going to be fun driving, anyway."

14

CHIEF SUPERINTENDENT JOHN BELLAMY turned from the window of his office overlooking the Embankment. "No, Grant," he said, "I do not think the Russians know that Herf is still alive. But they do not believe that a casual burglar strangled Herf's wife. They are convinced the three deaths are political assassinations."

"By British Intelligence?"

"Naturally they didn't say so, but that is probably what they are thinking."

"What was Zoya Alexandrovna's story?"

"She heard a noise and came down to investigate. She found Mrs. Mikoff on the floor, dead, a desk drawer pulled out and the french windows open. She thought she saw someone go out in the fog, but she isn't sure. She tried to revive Mrs. Mikoff, but realized she was dead. She called Poliski, an old man, very deaf, who seems to be butler-cum-general servant and is supposed to be some distant relation to the deceased woman. Between them they decided to inform the police and the Embassy. That's all. A nice, simple story with no loose ends."

"What did you think of the girl?"

"Good nerves, not easily scared and a convincing liar."

"She gives me the creeps. Did you find the passports?"

"No. There were a number of letters, written in German. I'd have taken them for examination, but the two Russians wanted them. In view of the evidence I couldn't very well refuse."

"I don't think they were important. But the passports were. Herf took them. Perhaps they were the reason for his return. What further information have you received from the Dutch police?"

"I've had a full report typed for you. Originally the Dutch knew him as Jan Weidmann, a native of Amsterdam. That was shortly before the war. During the war he vanished. He turned up again in Holland and was suspected of issuing forged money. For some reason his previous conviction was overlooked. No doubt their records were lost, or confiscated by the Germans. They got his finger-prints, but he eluded arrest. The next they heard of him was from the French police, through Interpol, only just getting into its stride in those days. Somehow he had learned the art of safe-breaking.

"One of the Dutchmen recognized his photograph as that of a man known to have collaborated with the Germans and who spied for them. His name was then Peter Zoram. The picture was given wide publicity in the Dutch and French newspapers. It yielded no results.

"Then came the affair of the American H.Q. theft and the man's arrest at the frontier and subsequent escape. His finger-prints were proved to be those of the original Jan Weidmann. After that, the finger-prints turned up all over the place, as I told you before."

"Yes, you did. But this new information doesn't get me any further," said Grant.

"It could do."

"How?"

"It shows how Herf first came to use a double. Herf must have seen those photographs in the papers and spent a very puzzled hour or so wondering why his photograph was being used. He must have come to the conclusion that here was an amazing coincidence. He would have done what the police failed to do, trace the man, because he would have realized the advantages of having a double at his service. Presumably his own finger-prints have never been recorded. But those of the other man were in the possession of both Dutch and French police and available to every nation in the world who cared to check. And, by the way, finger-prints on Herf's desk tally with those unidentified at Woolwich.

"One of the Dutch newspapers revealed the fact that the bank robber was known to have been a German spy. In effect, Weidmann had been officially identified as Herf. By using Weidmann when necessary Herf had the finest cover for himself that anyone could devise. If Weidmann was arrested and betrayed him no one would believe him. But the time came when Herf thought it wise to eliminate his double. Which suggests that he knew the game was growing too dangerous. Getting himself in with the Russians was probably an error he realized too late. He should have stayed on his own."

149

"This double business is an incredible coincidence," said Grant. "They must be related, and closely."

"Not at all," smiled Bellamy. "I personally have known at least one case of quite remarkable doubles who were in no way related. They were the same age, identical measurements, colouring, eyes, hair, skin, the lot. You couldn't tell them apart. Only their finger-prints were different. International police records are full of such cases. But with photographs only it is never possible to be absolutely sure. The Dutchman who recognized Weidmann as Herf couldn't possibly have remembered every little detail of the spy's face and body. But the whole taken together produced such a likeness that he had no hesitation in identifying his man. Could you have told the difference between the dead Weidmann and the living Herf from a casual inspection?"

"No," said Grant. "I could not. But what I'm interested in now is what other persons beside the Jap, Zidkov and Weidmann were operating with Herf in this affair, or other business. Something has slipped up with Herf's plans. I don't think he would stay in England otherwise. Have you got any further with the Jap's murder?"

"Not much."

"I'd like permission to search his premises."

Bellamy smiled: "If I say no, you'll soon find means of forcing my hand, eh?"

"No, no, we like to work amiably with the police."

"Why, of course. Yes, certainly you may search. I'll inform Barnard. What do you hope to find?"

Grant shrugged. "Who knows? Nothing in particular. I'm just hoping."

"There's nothing much any of us can do until we find Herf. Barnard is working hard to trace Weidmann's movements and contacts. If he gets a line I'll inform you at once."

Grant stayed with Bellamy for another twenty minutes talking over the case. But when he left he felt that he had made no progress towards tracing Herf or understanding the game the man was playing. The murder of his wife had been an accident forced upon him. Whatever Zoya Alexandrovna's position may have been before she now had a hold over him which she might seek to exploit.

Well, they had that covered. Zoya would be shadowed night and day. In the meantime, Winifredo Lecramberti might come up with something useful. It was a fascinating business, this gathering little bits of odds and ends of information and weaving them into a trap. That really was the basis of Intelligence work.

Grant telephoned Jenny that he was going to Woolwich. She told him Colonel Borlaise had returned and wanted to see him. So Grant postponed his exploration of the Jap's house and went to his H.Q.

Borlaise looked as hard and tough as ever, but his eyes were shadowed by fatigue. Grant guessed he hadn't had much sleep while he was in Paris.

He said: "I've read your report, Grant. What have you learned from Bellamy?"

Grant told him. Borlaise nodded: "I know about Weidmann. It looks as if we have Peter Herf on the run. But why?"

"He still has something uncompleted, sir. It may have been the passports. But I feel it is something more than that. Herf would not have left himself out on a limb without a passport."

"I agree it would be quite out of character. I'm going to suggest to you that the stolen documents are not in Herf's possession at all. What's more, he doesn't know where they are. He probably suspects, but he's not sure."

"Weidmann double-crossed him, so that's why he died?"

"Could be, but I don't like that as a theory, Grant. Weidmann must have known when he went to Woolwich that Herf and Zidkov would be waiting for him there."

"Zoya Alexandrovna lifted them from Weidmann, is that it, sir?"

"No, that can't be right. On your own showing she was concerned because Herf returned to his house. Her concern must have been for his safety, and probably her own. Whatever has happened, I think we can be sure Alexandrovna is still working with Herf. What she intends to do in the future is anybody's guess."

"She could be a Russian agent, set to trap Herf."

"When she must have helped him to escape?"

"Perhaps that was the only way she

hoped to recover the stolen documents. In any case, she hadn't much chance to hold a man of Herf's strength and weight. But I agree, the evidence is all against her collusion with the Russian security men. I don't know how she will stand up to the kind of inquisition she is bound to get from them. She's got a simple story, and she's got strong nerves. She may get away with it."

"What are you proposing to do at Woolwich, Grant?"

"Search for anything which might connect the Jap with Herf and any associates of whom we know nothing. I have no particular plans."

"The note-book you took from Herf's desk last night is the latest Russian military code as used in East Germany. I don't think the Russians would have trusted a mere C.R.O. in London with it. Nor would it have been necessary for him to know it. He must have stolen it. We have to find out more about this Pole, Eric Siloffski, the one the woman Lecramberti says she met in Paris and who had the tattooed eagle on his arm, like Herf. There is nothing in our records. I suppose she wasn't pulling a fast one on you, Grant?"

"I don't think so, but I wouldn't be certain."

"Women like that seldom speak the truth, unless they are made to."

"She's scared of deportation, sir."

"Then we will hold that over her. But you know how to handle her. Turn the screw until it hurts. Forget you're a gentleman. I've had the report on Porthy's desk. There was a secret compartment, very cleverly contrived in the back. It was empty. But it had been used very recently. According to the caretaker the desk is a new acquisition and is about the only piece of furniture in the flat that doesn't belong to the landlords. It is of Polish manufacture and some fifty years old."

"Do we know how Porthy came to have it?"

"The caretaker says it was brought there in a private car by a man who visited Porthy on several occasions and whom he thinks is a foreigner."

"The Pole who came to the flat with Herf and Zoya Alexandrovna," suggested Grant.

"Yes. We must know more about that Pole."

"I have the Lecramberti woman making inquiries, sir."

"Yes, you put that in your report. I hope she is discreet. We don't want to scare him off. I believe him to be Stephan Morizov, one-time major in the Polish Intelligence Corps. If it is the same man he is carrying on business as a secondhand furniture dealer in the Fulham area."

"Any record?"

"No. It appears to be a legitimate business. The police have nothing against him."

"Lecramberti said she met Herf again through this Pole. At a diplomatic party. She believed him to be a commercial agent for the Poles."

"Did she say what party?"

"No, sir."

"It may not have been a Polish Embassy party. In any case, it's easy for an intelligent man to gate-crash such a party, especially if he arrives late."

"You want me to vet him, sir?"

"No. Gilray can take on that job. You follow up what you've been doing. Bathic tried to get the truth from Porthy. He didn't get far. All he got was an admission that Alexandrovna had been to Porthy's flat and that he had helped Paul Fergus to dodge F.O. security before he bolted to Russia. Fergus was thick with Zoya Alexandrovna, too. Porthy telephoned the woman the night before he left, telling her when and how he was going to France. He declared she asked him. I don't know, Grant, Porthy was a queer fellow. Bathic was not the right man to have questioned him. We would have made a much better job. Well, that chance has gone."

"Was it suicide, sir?"

Colonel Borlaise shrugged: "It's gone on French police records as suicide. A woman saw him jump. But, of course, he could have been pushed. It doesn't matter now. We can't make him talk."

"Have we had Zidkov's letters from the C.I.D.?"

"Photostats. Jenny is working on them. They look to be harmless private correspondence from relatives in Russia. The police did all the standard tests, but they developed no secret writing. River water could have washed it out, I suppose. When the police have finished with them we'll do our own testing. Well, get off to Woolwich. I don't think you'll find anything. The Jap may have been in the drug traffic with Herf, but I doubt if he knew anything about Herf's espionage activities."

Grant stood up. He said: "I feel, sir, that the documents are still in this country."

"If they are not, I shudder to think what could happen. The F.O. must have been crazy to entrust a man like Porthy with them."

"Who gave Porthy his orders?"

"Bathic's secretary. I know what you're thinking. I'm watching that. All right. Report immediately if you find anything." Grant had reached the door when Borlaise said sharply. "Just one more thing, don't let any external influence fog your mind."

Grant paused and stared at him. He knew very well what the other meant.

"Such as, sir?" he asked.

"You don't want me to tell you. What happened to you last night that you let Herf go?"

"His arrest was a matter for the police. You agreed that, sir."

"There could have been an accident when you fought for the gun. That would have made sure he didn't escape."

"You forget Zoya Alexandrovna, sir."

"I do not forget her. Well, never mind, just remember what I've said."

"To what exactly are you referring, sir?" Grant's voice was polite but his eyes were hard.

"Jenny," snapped Borlaise. "I can't afford to lose either of you because you've grown soft. Forget it, Grant. Your duty is to me."

"When we have this Herf business settled, sir, I shall want to talk to you again."

"All right, but get the damned thing settled. I don't think you realize how serious it is."

"I do, sir. Whatever I may feel for Jenny will not interfere with my duty. Nor will it affect Jenny."

"I see. So it's got that far, has it?"

"It has, sir."

The granite face and hard eyes softened. His lips lengthened in something as near a smile as he ever achieved. "Grant, you make me sick," he declared. "I believed you to be woman-proof. Go on, get off to Woolwich before I tell you what I think of you . . . both."

15

GRANT WAS THINKING about the desk as he drove to Woolwich. It could well be that Porthy had not known of the secret compartment. Someone had suggested he wanted a desk, probably Zoya Alexandrovna and had offered him a desk as a present. It could have been dumped on him for use as a post-box or safe deposit unknown to him. She, or Herf, or some confederate, would have had access to the flat with the same type of master key as the girl had left behind when he had discovered her there.

Obviously she had been expecting to open the secret compartment when she' came to the flat. Somehow she had failed to find it and he had surprised her before she could do more. Perhaps he should have waited. But he wouldn't have learned any more because there was nothing to find in the compartment.

On balance, he felt that Porthy had been a weak fool, easily dominated by Paul

Fergus and later, Zoya Alexandrovna. He had fallen for the charm of an intelligent and unscrupulous woman who had used him for her own ends.

He thought of what the Old Man had said to him about Jenny. The final smile had softened the blow, but he was not deceived. Colonel Borlaise would make it difficult for them as he knew how. He was a man dedicated to his work. He wouldn't care a damn about their personal desires or feelings if they caused him any trouble.

Detective Inspector Trotter was just leaving the police station when Grant arrived.

"The Super ain't here," he said. "Mr. Bellamy phoned you were coming. Anything I can do?"

"I want to have another look at the Jap's premises."

"We gave it a real work over. What are you hoping to find that we missed?"

"I don't think you'd be likely to miss much, old timer. But we may not be looking for the same things."

"You'll be wasting your time. I picked up a nice lead from Sam Smelly. Remember him, the barrow boy?"

"Yes."

"He put us on to a dock rat named Kupper. We've had him several times for peddling reefers. He's cleared off somewhere, but we've got the drag out. His breed don't go far from home. Looks like we've uncovered something big in the drugs racket. Herf is in it. So was his double. We took enough stuff out of the Jap's store to dope half London. But I reckon there's a pile to find yet. Your best bet is through this racket. Herf'll be laid up with the gang somewhere. If he ain't slipped us and got across the water."

"Are you coming with me?" asked Grant.

"No, I'm a busy man. You carry on."

"How do I get in?"

Trotter laughed: "Same way as you did the first time."

"The door was open then."

"Like hell it was."

"Damn you, it was."

"All right, don't get heated. If I lend you the keys I have to send a constable with you. Do you want company?"

Grant smiled. "No. I'll manage."

"I bet you will, too," laughed Trotter. "Good luck. I wish I was a cloak and dagger boy. It must be fun."

Grant left his car at the police station and walked down to the antique shop. He used the same key as the one which had opened the door of Porthy's flat. He mounted the stairs with silent, cautious tread although he knew the place to be deserted.

All the doors had been locked by the police. He worked methodically through the rooms. But it was in the cubby-hole of an office at the back of the shop that he discovered two documents. One was an invoice carbon for an antique desk and crate of glass tumblers made out to Stephan Morizov at a Fulham address, and the other was a slip of paper in an accounts ledger which he recognized as written in the same code as he had found in Herf's desk.

He searched through all the bundles of invoices but this was the only one with Morizov's name upon it. As Morizov was a dealer in second hand furniture it might have no significance. Nevertheless he put it in his pocket together with the note in code. That would be something for the Old Man to work out.

It was mid-afternoon before he was satisfied that there was nothing more for him. He was about to pass out of the shop into the corridor below the stairs when he observed a man peering in at the windows. He stood back in the shadows and watched.

The man was tall, with a vaguely military bearing, well-dressed about forty-five years of age. Grant heard him try the shop door handle, pushing against the door when it failed to open. He slid out quickly and slid the bolt upon the side entrance. When he returned to the rear of the shop the man had gone. Then he heard him at the side door, inserting a key in the lock.

Grant stood back in case he looked through the letterbox and saw him. The man had discovered the bolt. What, he wondered, would happen next. If the man had any skill and the necessary equipment he would soon get a wire loop over the knob of the bolt.

But nothing happened. After five minutes Grant concluded he had given up the attempt. He slid the bolt, opened the door, and nearly bumped into the others back.

The man turned swiftly, half raising a hand in a defensive movement. He dropped it and gave Grant a rather sickly smile.

"Sorry," he said, "I was hoping to find the shop open."

Grant said nothing, staring at him with cold unfriendly eyes. The man moved his feet restlessly.

"You are not the proprietor?" It was more a statement than a question.

"I am a police officer," snapped Grant. "What do you want?"

"Oh, I see. Well, nothing. It was the picture. In the window. I rather wanted to buy it."

"The premises are closed. They will not reopen for a considerable time."

"Er . . . thank you." The man hesitated, took a few uncertain steps and then walked briskly away. Grant closed the door and followed down the road to the end of Hare Street, where the man crossed over and walked towards the Free Ferry.

It was then that Grant saw Gilray on the opposite side of the road walking down behind the man. He knew then that his hunch had been correct. The man was the Pole, Stephan Morizov. Gilray could, of course, be on a profitless venture, but he didn't think so.

He walked back to the police station and suggested to the station sergeant that a man should be put on to watch the antique shop.

"I'll mention it to Superintendent Barnard, sir."

"If Inspector Trotter comes in first, tell him," said Grant. "But can't you give the order?"

"Not with the Super on the job, sir."

Grant left it at that. He might have stayed and watched himself, but he didn't think Morizov would return in daylight, if he returned at all. If he thought the police were still in the house he wouldn't take that chance.

Driving back, Grant decided to take in Fulham on the way. He located the second hand furniture shop at last, chiefly by the huge picture in the side window, one identical with that exhibited in the antique shop at Woolwich.

He parked in a side street and walked back. The picture was the absolute twin of the other.

So what? he thought. It must mean

something. It can't be just coincidence.

He tried the door handle and found it unlocked. A bell gave a cracked tinkle as he walked in. A middle-aged woman, fat and oily, came out from a dark doorway at the rear.

"I'm interested in that picture," said Grant. "I'd like to buy it."

The woman had small, black eyes which looked like boot buttons in her pallid cheeks, which reminded Grant of a fat pig's face.

"I don't know you," she said, her voice thick and husky as if she suffered from some chronic throat complaint.

"No, of course you don't know me," said Grant. "Does it matter?"

"You come back when the boss is home, mister," she retorted. "I'm only looking after the place while he's out."

"When will that be?"

"I don't know. Late, perhaps."

"How late?"

"Don't ask me. I don't know. He didn't say."

Grant thanked her politely and walked out. The picture was in the window for the purpose of identifying the premises. The

167

most probable explanation was that it was a sign for drug addicts. If he searched he would probably find others in similar shops scattered over London. There would be a central office. The addicts would be directed to these depots, probably never the same place twice running. It was a bright idea, but it only required one squeal to the police and the whole structure fell. He would leave it to the Old Man whether the information was passed on to the Metropolitan Police or not.

Jenny was in the outer office when Grant returned. She said: "We've had word that Herf may be laid up in a dope joint in Poplar. The Old Man wants to see you. Did you have any luck?"

"Some, I think. I'll tell you when I've seen the Old Man."

Jenny took up an inter-office telephone and dialled a number. She said: "Ian Grant is here." She put the instrument on its cradle and smiled: "Go right ahead."

Grant leaned over and kissed her as he passed.

Colonel Bolaise signed him to a chair and pushed cigarettes towards him. It looked as if it might be a long session.

"Well?" he demanded.

"Two things only," said Grant, "these papers. One in code. The other an invoice to Stephan Morizov."

He gave his verbal report as Borlaise studied the two pieces of paper. He put them aside as Grant concluded.

"So Morizov called at the Jap's shop. He must know that the man was murdered. Did he actually cross the river?"

"He went down to the landing stage. There was a ferry coming alongside. But I didn't wait. I saw Gilray on his tail."

"I'll talk to Bellamy about the picture, Grant. I think you are on to something there, but I don't see that it helps us too much with Herf. However, with any luck we may get him tonight."

"So we know where he is?"

"Yes. Barnard picked up one of the small fry, a specimen named Kupper. He talked fast. Herf is laid up in a gambling joint in Poplar, near the docks, a place frequented by foreign seamen and their molls. The divisional C.I.D. men know what it is, but two raids have failed to establish a case. You know what it's like. By the time they've got the door open there's not a gambling device to be found, just a few seamen and women playing harmless games of cards or just sitting around drinking. The rest, and the equipment, vanish into thin air."

"How do they hope to be more successful tonight?" asked Grant.

Borlaise smiled, rather a grim smile.

"That's where you come in."

"Me? How?"

"You will be the pilot. You will go as a German seaman and gain admittance. When you have sized up the place and all the snags you will then admit the police, secretly."

Grant laughed: "Just like that, sir."

Borlaise shrugged. "You've done more difficult things, Grant. Frankly, I don't believe this will be difficult at all. Your German is perfect. You're good at the low life character. I don't think there will even be much risk."

Like hell, thought Grant, but said nothing. Borlaise went on:

"In your character as a German seaman you will wait for Barnard and his men in the saloon bar of 'The White Duck' in Bertin Street. When he is ready you will proceed to the club and get in. Barnard will fix the details with you. Right?"

"Yes, indeed. It should be interesting. What do I do if I see Herf?"

"Make sure he's in no condition to escape this time, Grant."

"Surgeon or undertaker?"

"Surgeon. We want him alive. He has a lot to tell us."

"I'll do my best," said Grant.

"No man can do more. I'll fix papers for you. Now let's see what this note says."

Colonel Borlaise took out a code book and began to work on the paper Grant had taken from the ledger. Grant lit another cigarette and waited, thinking of the task which had been given him. It could prove relatively easy, but it was more likely not to be. Unless Barnard had come into possession of the pass-word the first moments would be awkward, and might ruin the whole show. He wondered if the grim-faced superintendent had asked for him, or if the Old Man had suggested it. More probably the latter. Grant smiled as he thought of something that would shake him.

Borlaise looked up. He said, reading:

"*Nippon,* Tilbury, twenty-seventh. Yusa red silk three bales."

He reached for the telephone, the direct outside line, turning over the pages of a note-book he had taken from a drawer. Grant watched him dialling, trying to determine the letters and numbers, a thing he often did when watching others telephoning. It was something which could prove useful one day. In this game you never knew what odd bit of information or accomplishment might not some day prove important. He had learned to lip read for this very reason.

Borlaise asked: "Will you please tell me when the *Nippon* docks at Tilbury." He waited a couple of minutes then said, "Thank you." He looked at Grant. "The *Nippon* from Japan. The red silk will be stiff with drugs. However, if we get Herf tonight that'll be a matter for the police. Go well armed, Grant. Arm and leg holsters. Wear a knife, too. Carry some trilene and a pad of cotton wool. You may need to keep Herf quiet."

Grant smiled. "I thought you said it would be easy, sir."

"Well, you never know how events may

turn. Just as easy to go prepared for the worst."

Grant nodded. He said quietly: "I think it would be an idea to take a woman with me. I suggest Jenny. She has good strong nerves and is an accomplished actress. She'd be a great help."

The Old Man's hard eyes glinted like steel.

"No," he said. "I have work for Jenny. In any case, it will not help you to be burdened with a woman."

"It was just an idea, sir."

"And a damned bad one, too!"

Grant wanted to laugh, but he kept a straight face. The Old Man had risen to the bait. He had not the slightest intention of risking Jenny's life in such a venture. But he did want to observe the other's reactions to such a suggestion.

"I'm sorry, sir."

"So you ought to be. All right. That's all. Get yourself fixed up. Be in that pub around nine-thirty. And remember, I'm counting on you. I want Herf, and alive. But I'd rather have him dead than not at all."

As Grant was rising to leave the telephone rang on the desk. Borlaise answered. He said: "Keep watching," and put down the instrument. "That was Gilray. The Pole went into the gambling joint and is still there. So that definitely links him with Herf, either drugs or documents, maybe both. However, he's not your bird, so you don't have to bother about him, even if he's on the premises when you get in."

Grant went out to Jenny. "Let's slip out for tea," he said. "Then I must get a couple of hours sleep. I fancy I'm in for a busy night."

16

IT WAS EXACTLY at half past nine that Grant pushed open the swing doors of the saloon bar of 'The White Duck' and stepped into an atmosphere thick with tobacco smoke and the reek of beer. He was dressed in a blue double-breasted suit of nautical cut, made in Hamburg, with a well worn uniform peaked cap pulled low over his eyes. Injections in the lobes of his ears had enlarged them. A rubber plug in one nostril gave his nose a twisted, battered appearance, enhanced with a purple tinge, which also extended to his cheeks, a sign of the heavy drinker.

When he ordered a beer it was in English, but with a guttural German accent. He leaned against the bar and surveyed the customers, mostly seamen and dock rats with a number of ladies of the town. No one took any notice of him.

A young woman in the uniform of the Salvation Army came in selling copies of the *War Cry*. Grant watched her, thinking that she had courage to visit such a place. She came up to him, but in his character of a German seaman he shrugged and shook his head. She said softly: "Be in the yard behind in ten minutes. Mr. Barnard is waiting for you." She moved to the swing doors, opened them and went out. Grant thought he hadn't lost his capacity for surprise. She was, he supposed, a woman police officer, but he would never have suspected it.

In the darkness of the yard Grant met Barnard. With him was the Sub-Divisional Detective Chief Inspector, whom he introduced as Coleman. It was the Chief Inspector who did the talking.

"It's a corner building up here on the right. It's run by a Jamaican named Martineau. He's got eight or nine toughs, mostly coloured, as his bodyguards and chuckers-out. Just about now it'll be warming up for the night. It's a private club, so we haven't been able to do much about it, the law being what it is. My information is that the password now in current use is 'Looks like fog.' But I don't suppose that keeps out people they know if they haven't the current password."

"Have you the names of any members whom you know are not around tonight?" asked Grant.

"Yes. There's a German named Ramler and an Italian named Lugi Vittori, both doing stretches and recently convicted. Ramler is in Wandsworth and Vitorri in Dartmoor. There's Kupper, too. He won't be there tonight. Maybe he's your best alibi, if you need one."

"What force have you?"

"Adequate, sir. The place will be surrounded. Once you've been inside and got the present lay-out and the doors open, then in we come. But I warn you, don't take any chances. They'd cut your throat or stab you in the back without a moment's hesitation. And we'd never find your corpse."

"Thanks, Chief," smiled Grant. "I'm looking forward to it."

"Well, better get started, sir. If we wait, the place will be crowded. We don't want too much of a bloody battle."

Grant walked up the dark, dismal street until he came to the house. He descended the area steps and thumped on the door. A grill slid open and a black face looked out.

"What do you want, mister?" demanded the negro.

"I play," said Grant in his guttural voice.

"I don't know you, mister. You clear off."

Grant let go a foul oath in German.

"Open," he demanded. "I am told to come here. I play, you understand."

Grant's voice was loud. The doorkeeper didn't want to attract police attention. He opened the door. Two other strong-arm men were waiting in the corridor as Grant lurched in. They looked an ugly pair. One said aggresively: "You're a stranger. Who sent you?"

"Kupper."

"What sort of night is it?"

"Looks like fog."

"O.K." nodded the strong-arm, "sign him in."

The doorman pushed a block of membership forms towards Grant and a ballpointed pen. Grant said: "You fill it in. I can't read English." He smacked a German mariner's ticket on the small table. "That is my name."

"Ah, what the hell!" exclaimed the door-keeper. "Go on, mister. It ain't necessary. You be my guest." He couldn't read English either.

Grant pocketed his mariner's card and moved on towards the door at the end of the corridor. When he pushed open the door he was surprised at the size and loftiness of the room, and the number of people present.

A very large negro stood inside the door. His dark eyes regarded Grant in a quick, estimating stare. Grant gave him a surly scowl and moved into the room. The negro took no further interest in him. He went over to the table where a crowd was gathered, playing faro, a game of pure chance, requiring no skill. It is just a gamble on the turn of the cards as they come up through an opening in the top of a box fixed to the table. The players back their fancy on a sheet painted with the thirteen cards of each suit.

If the game is operated honestly it is just a plain gamble, but a skilled operator can flip up almost any card in the pack he wants to beat the odds. This would be part of the profits, but Grant guessed that the money was really made on the sale and distribution of drugs. This place might well be the central office of the traffic.

He watched the game. Dead silence prevailed as the box showed the winning card. Immediately afterwards there was a rush of talk. The players seemed to be drawn from every part of the world, but were mainly seamen. Here and there he saw men well dressed, perhaps adventurers from more respectable quarters. As yet there were very few women.

He thought of the chief inspector's warning. He was right. They were a tough-looking mob. He didn't want to stay too long before he got down to business. If Herf, or Morizov, were on the premises they wouldn't be among this crowd.

Grant began to move towards the door at the far end, stopping to stake a bet at each of the other two tables where play was in progress. He lost both times. No one took any notice of him. Gamblers believe in lucky places. If they thought about him at all it would be that he was seeking his lucky spot.

Presently he reached the door and leaned against it, testing it with his shoulder as he lit a long black cheroot. The door was not locked and worked on an automatic spring. When the faro game at the nearest table was at its most tense moment he slid out.

A low-powered, fly-blown electric lamp shed a feeble glow along a stone-paved corridor. He moved along it to a flight of stairs. Below the stairs a sign read, euphemistically, "Gentlemen." He paused. The lavatory door opened and a man came out, pushing past him, ascending the stairs with long strides. Grant recognized the big body and hard face of Peter Herf.

He decided against further exploration of the premises. He could do that when the police were in. He returned to the faro room, worked his way slowly across it, watching until the negro bodyguard's attention was diverted, and went out quickly.

With swift silent tread he came up behind the doorkeeper and cut him stiff-handed across the neck. The man dropped like a pole-axed cow. Grant laid him clear and opened the door. At the top of the area steps Detective Chief Inspector Coleman was waiting in the shadows.

"The door's open," whispered Grant.

"Come in. I'm going back. I've seen Herf."

"Wait, sir," advised Coleman. "This could be very rough."

"That's why I want to get back. I'd hate to have Peter Herf slip us."

"The place is surrounded, sir. No one can get away."

"Herf has done it before, Chief. Don't worry about me. I'm well armed."

Grant went down the steps again, along the corridor and into the faro room. This time the big negro was not there. He saw him on the other side of the room where some sort of dispute was taking place. Perhaps the operator had been a little clumsy in flipping up the right card to beat the table and someone had accused him of cheating. Which, Grant thought, would be a very foolhardy thing for any man to do in such company.

He reached the door and passed through into the corridor. With his habitual caution he began to mount the stairs to a wide landing, uncarpeted, floored with dirty wooden blocks. A number of doors, all closed, stood in a row before him.

The sounds of the faro room came up like a murmur of the sea. But somewhere close to him he heard another sound, a man groaning. He listened intently, deciding that the sounds came from the room with the door immediately to his right. He eased over and gripped the handle. The door was not locked. When he opened it gently an inch or so he heard the groaning very distinctly.

Flashing his torch Grant looked in. The room was absolutely bare of furniture, but stretched on the floor was a man, whose face was a bloody mess, as if he had been beaten-up without mercy. He stepped in and knelt by the man. He recognized him by his clothes, Stephan Morizov, the Pole whom he had seen at Woolwich earlier in the day.

Morizov was in a bad way. He might even be dying. Grant leaned over and slipped up the sleeve of his right arm. He saw it then, the tattooed eagle, identical with the other.

So intent was he on his discovery that he missed the faint creak behind him. He was just that split second too late. The rubber cosh took him across the skull in a blinding flash of agony and he fell across the groaning Morizov, unconscious.

From down below came the roar of noise as pandemonium broke loose in the faro room. Superintendent Barnard and the police were in.

17

IAN GRANT CAME to consciousness in total darkness, aware only at first that he felt very ill. He wondered what had happened to him and for several minutes he lay quite still, his head feeling as if it would explode with the pain of the sledge-hammer blows. A sudden attack of acute nausea took him. He struggled blindly to his knees and was violently sick. When it had finished he fell back exhausted. But the terrible hammering in his head had ceased leaving only a dull ache.

With the easing pain memory returned in a swift flash of mental illumination. He was Herf's prisoner. It was not a happy thought. He found a moment in which to marvel that he was still alive.

What had happened to the police raid? That, apparently, had been a failure. He thought of what Colonel Borlaise had said, that he relied on him. Too bad!

He began to take a more intelligent interest in his own position. His hands and feet were free. That was something. His pistol had gone from his shoulder holster, but the holster was still in position. His belt and knife were gone. So was the bottle of trilene, but the cotton-wool pad had been left. Very carefully he sat up and felt over his left shin. A thrill of satisfaction rippled through him, the .22 Spanish automatic was still there. Whoever had searched him had missed it.

Where was he? In a cellar, it seemed, somewhere very near the river because he could hear the muffled hooting of the tugboats. And the smell, too. Slowly and painfully he hauled himself to his feet, anxious not to start that headache rioting again. He began to traverse the cellar. It took him only a minute to realize how small it was. But there was a very substantial door, which, he thought, was bolted on the outside, because he could find no keyhole. Not that it would have helped him very much. He had no tools with him.

That he was in a desperate position was all too plain. But the knowledge did not dismay him. He had been in some pretty hopeless situations before and come out of them without much hurt. At least he had the neat little .22 pistol to comfort him.

He leaned against the damp, slimy wall and thought of Jenny. He hoped she wasn't too worried about his disappearance. One thing was certain, whatever the Old Man said, or thought, she would force him to make some attempt at rescue.

He heard the sound of a heavy bolt being drawn and braced himself. A light showed as the door opened and a powerful torch shone full into his eyes. He turned his head and snarled in German. "Keep that light away, damn you." He closed his eyes to mere slits, half-blinded by the glare. He could just make out the shadowy forms by the open door.

He recognized the voice when Herf spoke, even though it was in German. "Ah, so you are recovered. Who the devil are you?"

"I could ask you that question," snarled Grant. "Where am I?"

"I want an answer," declared Herf, quietly, but with deadly menace in its level tones.

"Hans Mulheim, of Hamburg."

"A seaman?"

"Yes."

"What ship?"

"The *Gottlieb*."

"She sailed three days ago."

"Don't I know it. The bastards left me behind. I was drunk, I suppose. Now, let me out of here. Somebody coshed me. I feel like death. I want a drink."

"What were you doing upstairs at the Eagle Club?"

"Looking for money. I'm near broke."

"Do you always go armed like a bandit?"

Grant snarled a German oath, very foul. "What if I do?"

"I find it interesting. How long have you been at sea?"

"Too long."

"That's not an answer."

"That's all you'll get. And put that gun away. It doesn't scare me. Who the hell are you anyway? Do you always have to have a bodyguard?"

"Not always. Have you got a police record?"

"I've been around. I don't like police any more than you do, I reckon. What's the big idea keeping me here?"

"I might have work for you, when I've checked. In the meantime you stay here."

Grant made a step forward. The torch beam centred on his eyes, checking him. He heard the door close. His head was aching again. That damned light was like a white hot flame in his eyes. He felt in his pocket. The German mariner's card had been taken. He couldn't be sure that he had deceived Herf. If he had means of checking he would soon discover that Hans Mulheim had sailed with his ship, outward bound for Cape Town. But it seemed most unlikely that Herf would be able to check. That was bluff while he decided what was best to be done with him.

Cramped and chilled, Grant moved around in the darkness. Wherever he stood in the cellar it was damp. Water actually dripped down one wall, which was probably right on the river bank. He was very thirsty and at odd moments he had a return of the nausea.

Presently he was aware of a faint grey light filtering through the darkness and realized that there was a tiny opening high up in one wall, the one that dripped water. Day was dawning outside. The thought filled him with new hope and determination.

He wondered how long Herf intended to keep him in the cellar, and why. If he was satisfied with his identity as a stranded German seaman he might offer him a job within his organization. He thought of the eagle tattooed on Morizov's arm. The Pole had had a severe beating-up. Again he asked himself why.

A sound came to him, filtering through the grilled hole high up in the wall. The river water actually lapped against the wall of the cellar. He tried to think when it would be the next high tide. What if it rose above the level of the wall vent? He would be drowned like a rat in a trap. But after a few moment's of uneasy consideration he decided that was not Herf's idea, or was it? He seemed to specialise in death by drowning, no marks of violence on the bodies. He tried to dismiss the thought from his mind, but several times he found himself glancing towards that hole in the wall, growing brighter with the increasing daylight.

Grant judged it to be about eleven o'clock when he heard the bolts being drawn back again. He slipped the tiny automatic pistol from his shin holster and stood behind the door. The big negro he had seen in the faro room came in, a jug of water in his left hand and a loaf of bread under his arm. In his right hand he held a Luger pistol. Grant shot him through the hand and as the Luger fell with a clatter to the stone floor he cut stiff handed across the negro's throat. The man's mouth fell open. The jug dropped and shattered. Grant smashed in a left to the solar-plexus, paralyzing the nerve centre and as the negro crumpled cut him again across the neck. He could have killed the man with that cut, but the negro was tough. He went down on his knees and it took a kick to the chin to put him out.

Grant turned him over. He was wearing a leather belt and a bandana. He bound his arms behind his back with the belt, bracing it tightly. He slipped off the bandana, stuffed the cotton-wool pad he still had in his pocket in the man's mouth and bound it there with the bandana. He unfastened the trousers and pulled them down about his ankles, refastening them so that if he managed to rise he would have great difficulty in stepping out of them.

A search of the pockets revealed nothing but a wallet stuffed with money. He left it. The bullet had ploughed through the first finger joint and was still lodged somewhere in the hand, but he was not bleeding seriously.

He picked up the Luger, checked it over, found the magazine full and one in the barrel, and slipped it into his shoulder holster. For a couple of minutes the nausea took him again, but he fought down the sickening sensation and prepared to move out. The china jug smashing on the stone had made the most noise, but he doubted if it would have been heard.

Bolting the door on the unconscious negro, Grant stepped silently along a stone paved passage, damp and slippery. He came to a short flight of stone steps. At the top was a door, standing open. A wide passage ran either way. At the far right end was a small window. Grant turned that way, moving as swiftly as he dared, putting his feet down cautiously to avoid any noise. He had covered half the distance to the window when a door opened and a man stepped out. Grant's Luger snapped up, pointing straight at the man, who was short, thick-set, clad in a double-breasted blue suit very similar to the one he was wearing himself.

"Put 'em up," snarled Grant, motioning with the pistol.

The man raised his hands. Grant went down his pockets, searching for a weapon. He found none.

"Now lead the way out of this place," he ordered.

But the man made no movement. It occurred to Grant that he didn't understand English. He repeated the order in German. The man turned slowly, reluctantly, and began to walk down the passage towards the window.

Grant stepped close behind him, the Luger pressed against his spine. They had almost reached the window, where he observed another flight of stairs going up, when a voice spoke suddenly behind him, in German.

"Stop, or I'll kill you."

He recognized that voice. He whirled, crouched and fired, He saw Herf's gun flash and felt the tug at his sleeve as the bullet ripped through. The German at his side cried out, dropped his hands and staggered against the wall, grasping his thigh.

Grant turned and raced up the stairs. At

the turn he checked, crouched and waited. He heard Herf shouting orders and the sound of running feet in the passage below. Then Herf's head appeared at the bottom of the stairs and Grant shot to kill. But even as he squeezed the trigger Herf's head disappeared and his bullet hit the wall to ricochet with ringing violence.

Grant moved back and stood upright, surveying the stairs above. If he didn't go he would be trapped between two lines of fire. He went swiftly up and came to another passage identical with the one below.

He heard footsteps on the stairs and above him. They were moving in for the kill. He opened the first door he saw, dived into the room and closed and locked the door. Except for an odd assortment of lumber the place was unfurnished. With desperate urgency he began to pile the boxes, a broken chair, and spars of wood against the door. It might give him the few extra seconds he needed.

He crossed the room to the window, opened it and looked out. Below him was the river, with not a single ship, barge or tug within sight. The drop was a full fifty feet. He had never had any head for heights and it made him feel sick. Just outside the window a rain water pipe ran up the wall. It looked like a choice between that and a jump. He preferred the pipe. If it tore away he'd still have his jump.

A bullet smashed through the door lock, urging him on, making up his mind for him. He scrambled up, got his hands on the pipe and gave it a tug. It seemed solid enough. He swung himself out upon the sill, hesitated, conquering a dreadful urge to look down, and let his weight pull upon the pipe.

Climbing it was easier than he had expected, but when he reached the top where the pipe joined the guttering he had his moment of near panic. The metal trough was old and loose.

His fingers were cramped and the muscles of his arms and abdomen felt as if they were being torn apart. He let go with one hand reached up, putting pressure on the guttering. Next moment the whole section swung down, just missing his head, and struck him upon the shoulder. A shower of grit and slimy water descended upon his face, half blinding him, pouring over the pipe, making it so slippery that he nearly lost his hold. He brought his hand back and hung on, while everything spun round him in a nightmare whirl. The pipe appeared to have taken on the quality of india-rubber, while the walls swayed as if they were about to crumble and fall.

Grant conquered the urge to let himself fall and be done with it. Blindly he groped upwards for a handhold, found a concrete ridge below the slates and began to haul himself up. How he accomplished that last drag of his body over the ledge he never knew. It was the crash of the pistol below him which had probably given him the strength. At that moment the guttering had torn away and fallen.

The roof went up in an easy slope. Slowly, painfully, he crawled away from the ledge and reached the angle of the roof. He lay across it, exhausted, bathed in perspiration, feeling the tremble in his limbs. It had been a near thing and he knew it.

Presently he recovered. Below him on the other side was a flat roof, flanked by the walls of taller buildings. If he could find a skylight into another building he might have a fair chance of escape. But did he want to escape? His job was to get Herf. There would be no hope of bringing the man out, so he had to make up his mind what he was going to do, seriously wound him, or kill him.

The odds were that he wouldn't do either. Herf and his gang would get him first.

He wondered what had induced him to make that lunatic climb, when it would have been so much quicker, and safer, to have gone down the pipe. At the back of his mind must have been the idea that Herf would naturally conclude he had gone down, and escaped. Well, that idea had proved a dead loss. Herf, or someone, had seen him and shot at him before he made that last fearful scramble to the roof. So they knew where to find him.

Grant was sliding down the roof slope when the heavy clouds which darkened the sky broke in a deluge of rain. It beat upon his head with increasing violence, soaking him before he had gained what little shelter the flat roof below offered.

He found a skylight close against the near wall, an eighteen-inch square of glass set in a wooden frame. When he got his finger tips under the rim and heaved the skylight remained as firm as rock. He glanced around the flat roof, lashed with the blinding rain. Blank walls hemmed him in. If he didn't get the skylight open he was trapped as effectively as he had been in the cellar.

He tried again, but he could not move it. If he hoped to get in, now was the time, with the lash of rain to deaden some of the noise. He raised a foot and stamped with his heel on the glass. It fell with a crashing sound which seemed loud enough to be heard all over the building. When he looked in he saw nothing but a grey void beneath him. He began to stamp out the jagged pieces of glass sticking to the frame. It would be a tight enough squeeze getting through without the additional hazard of glass.

Grant looked at the hole. He doubted if he could ease his big body through. The frame would have to come out. He got a foot in and kicked with his heel. On the third attempt the frame moved. When he kicked again it came up intact. The hole was now large enough. He knelt down and peered in, but he couldn't be sure what sort of drop lay below him. It was a chance he had to take.

He swung his feet and legs through and lowered himself. At the full stretch of his arms he felt the floor under his toes and let go his hold. As far as he was able to determine he was in a bare room, an attic, which smelled damp and musty. Probably the flat roof leaked.

The door was unlocked. Outside was a small landing and steep, narrow stairs. Testing each step he went slowly down to a corridor below. Light from a window at the end filtered through in a pale grey illumination which barely relieved the shadows. He was about to move along the corridor when he heard a voice speak, in German. Grant eased back and crouched on the lower stair.

"What are we going to do with that shipment of hemp?"

A second voice spoke. Grant recognized it as that of Herf, and felt the excitement stir in his blood. Herf answered:

"Probably we shall have to abandon it."

"You have to find that man, Peter."

"I know. You don't have to tell me," Herf's voice was harsh, even angry.

"We cannot delay more than another three days."

"I'll find him."

"He was probably a British agent."

"No, he was a damned slick pickpocket, my dear Hans. I have a good idea where he is to be found."

"What of the thief who broke into your house? I do not believe in coincidence."

"He was just a plain kitchen burglar. I saw the man. I know. If he had been a British agent he would not have run away from Zoya. You see phantoms where none exist, Hans."

It was stupid, but Grant felt a small thrill of satisfaction that he had deceived Herf. The German spoke again:

"I will meet you at the house of Stephan Morizov. I think you were too severe with him, Peter. There was no need to have hurt him so much."

"Morizov is a menace," retorted Herf. "Sometimes I wonder if he is not a damned spy among us. He needed a lesson. He got it. I think it would be wiser if you did not go to his house."

"How then shall we meet?"

"I will insert a message in the personal

column of the *Telegraph*. I have a feeling Morizov must go."

"He has served us well."

"So did the others. But they were not of the breed we are, Hans. They served us only for money. Now go, before the police track us to this place. They are much too close for comfort."

"What of the German sailor?"

"He can stay on the roof. If he talks to the police he will be too late. My guess is he will keep his mouth shut."

"How do you know he's not a British agent?"

"I don't. What does it matter who he is? Now, you'd better go."

"I don't like it, Peter," declared the other. "Things have gone wrong. I feel we should cut our losses and quit while we are able. Are those documents so valuable?"

"Yes. I intend to get them. And I shall. So do not worry, my dear Hans. Look for my advertisement in the newspaper."

Grant wondered what he ought to do. He heard footsteps go along the corridor, only one man. Herf was still there. One thing stood out a mile, Herf had either lost the documents or had never had them. The extent of Herf's activities in this country were greater than the Old Man knew. If they got Herf they might miss the rest. But his instructions were to get Herf, dead or alive.

He heard heavy steps pounding upstairs and along the corridor. A voice cried in German: "The place is surrounded by police. They are breaking-in."

Herf said calmly: "So soon? Very well, Freudel, you know what to do. Hurry."

The heavy feet went away in a run. Grant stepped out. He heard a door close, but he was in time to see which one. He drew his Luger and turned the handle. The door opened. In the grey light he saw a room furnished like an office, but there was no one there.

A large door in a built-in cabinet suggested the exit. When he tried to open it he failed. With a sickening feeling that Herf had eluded him once again Grant ran out and down the stairs. Below was a corridor similar to the one above. He went quickly to the window, opened it and looked out upon the dark, oily water of the river flowing under a wharf.

Whatever he might have decided to do

he had no time. There came a sudden roar, a blinding sheet of flame from the other end of the corridor and a second later he was hurled bodily through the open window to hit the water with a dull splash.

18

IAN GRANT STIRRED uneasily. Somewhere near him voices were speaking. In a dim, unreal way he realized it, but he was tired, so tired that he made no effort to listen. He was aware of a gentle rocking motion and settled himself more comfortably. A voice spoke close to him. "He's tough. He'll be all right. Lucky we picked him up so soon."

Grant roused himself to a more intelligent interest in himself. Memory returned, vague at first, but sufficient to disturb his comfort. He remembered that he had been in danger, but he could not recollect just what it was. The voice. He knew he ought to know it. He opened his eyes and saw the man looking down at him. The man spoke. "That's better, sir. You took a nasty crack on the head when you came sailing out of that window. Hit one of the wharf piles. Damned lucky for you we were coming alongside, or you'd have drowned."

He remembered then. This was Inspector Gregory of the Thames Division of the Metropolitan Police. He remembered the explosion, too.

"What caused the blast?" he asked.

"As a guess I'd say they had explosives stored there and either accidentally or deliberately fired them."

"It was deliberate. I heard Herf give the order. What happened to him?"

"I wouldn't know, sir. We had a couple of boats standing off, just in case any attempt was made to escape by water. But you were the only fish we caught. How are you feeling?"

"Very tired."

"Did you have a rough time?"

"Yes, not so good."

"Well, there's a doctor waiting for you. We'll be alongside in a few minutes."

"I don't want a doctor," protested Grant.

"Mr. Bellamy's orders, sir."

So Bellamy had been there, too. Grant said no more. He thought of Colonel Borlaise, and Jenny. They would be glad he had escaped alive, but for very different reasons. That Herf had been killed in the explosion was too much to expect. But police officers might well have died or been seriously injured.

"Were any of your men hurt ?" he asked.

"I don't think so," said Gregory. "No one had got in before the explosion. The place was set alight. Anyone left inside would have died, I fancy."

Grant thought of Stephan Morizov. What had happened to him? The odds were Herf had left him, if he had been brought there from the gambling club. If he had not, then the police would have got him.

The launch came alongside. A man carrying a black bag jumped aboard and stepped into the cabin.

"Hello, Doc," said Gregory, "here's your patient."

"I'm all right," declared Grant. "Damned tired, that's all."

The doctor, a middle-aged man with a great deal of varied experience, smiled: "All the same, I'll make sure before we turn you loose."

Grant allowed himself to be examined.

"No," said the doctor, "there's nothing wrong with you that a good sleep will not cure. I can't help feeling that you've been very lucky. Chief Superintendent Bellamy is at the station. He wants to see you. I have my car. I'll take you along."

Bellamy was in the C.I.D. room when Grant walked in. He gave him a smile as they shook hands.

"I thought you'd bought a one-way ticket this time, Grant," he said.

"So did I. Herf got away, I suppose?"

"I'm afraid so. There is an underground passage, an old sewer, connecting those two buildings. But we got Stephan Morizov."

"Alive?"

"Only just. However, he has talked a little. He'll pull through and then we'll get a statement. He's full of hate."

"What did he say?"

"Something more of interest to you than to me. The tattooed eagle is a sign of a secret society pledged to restore the old order in Poland. Most of the members are ex-army officers of Polish-German origin. Herf is a man of aristocratic blood who was more or less a founder-member, but took no active part until recently. He married the sister of a high-up in the Russian Communist Inner Circle in the character of Mikoff."

"I don't understand how that was possible," said Grant. "He must have had fantastic luck and taken tremendous risks."

"He met the sister in America. Probably the original Mikoff was a Russian-American and Herf knocked him off and assumed his identity. Zoya Alexandrovna is a Russian-American. Maybe she helped him."

"What part did Morizov play in all this?"

"Morizov was a member of the secret society of the eagle. But he knew it was a hopeless ideal and quit when he came to England. Herf discovered him and forced him into the drug racket, which he declared was simply a means of raising funds for the society. That's his story, anyway. It could be true. Herf made a mistake in beating him up so much. Morizov is now in a state of mind when he has only one idea, to get even with Herf."

"A very agreeable state for us." smiled Grant. "Did he reveal any other names?"

"Several. I have sent a report to Colonel Borlaise. He's coming down here. Now, if you are not too exhausted, I'd like your story."

"I'm not exhausted," said Grant. "Just in need of sleep."

Bellamy listened to him with close attention. When he had concluded, he smiled: "You certainly had it rough! Do you think there's anything in the pickpocket idea?"

"Yes."

"It seems improbable, Grant. How would a casual pickpocket work on a man like Herf?"

"In the fog, why not?"

"Yes, of course, I was forgetting the fog. All the same, I don't like it much."

"You can check up on every known dip in London."

"I'll do that, certainly."

"What don't you like about it?"

"The coincidence."

"Yes, I agree. But if the dip whipped Herf's wallet, passport and papers as well as the documents, that might account for his returning to his house. Zoya Alexandrovna was astonished at his folly. Herf must have had an exceedingly good reason for taking such a risk."

Bellamy nodded. "Well, I'll check on all the known dips. I can't help feeling it must have been one of the top boys, if your theory is right."

"If Herf finds him first you'll have another murder on your hands."

"I'm thinking of that too."

"Morizov said nothing about the stolen F.O. papers, eh?"

"No. I doubt if he knows much about Herf's activities, or his contacts. I think he's an honest man who was blackmailed into helping Herf. But I could be wrong. With a man in that state it's difficult to judge. But I feel sure when he does make a full statement it will be a true one."

"Why do you think Herf set the place alight?"

"Probably because he had a lot of drugs stored there. We shall know more about that when we search the ruins. He might have had arms, too. They would be needed if a revolt was contemplated. A crazy idea, anyway. They must be a mad lot. Herf was using them as his pawns to build up his own fortunes."

"Where will you start searching for Herf now?"

Bellamy shrugged. "Someone will talk. We got a nice bunch in the raid. Herf is on the run. He can't escape us."

Grant hoped the chief superintendent's confidence was justified. He had his own ideas what Herf would do and he was anxious to talk to the Old Man about them.

Fifteen minutes later Colonel Borlaise arrived at the police station.

19

THE RINGING OF the telephone awakened
Grant. He glanced at the clock. He had
slept for six hours. The soft, seductive
voice of Winifredo Lecramberti came
whispering over the wires.

"Ian, darling, I have news for you. Come
along and see me as soon as possible."

"Is it that urgent?" he asked.

"It could be. I don't want to tell you
over the telephone, darling. Can't you
come now, tonight?"

"All right. I'll be with you within the
hour."

"I shall be counting the seconds, darling."

Grant heard the instrument click at the
other end of the line. He lifted the
"scrambler" and waited. Gilray's voice
answered him.

"Put me through to Jenny or the Old
Man," said Grant.

"Neither here. The Old Man is with
Bellamy at the Yard. Jenny is off duty,
probably at home. Anything I can do?"

"Just record that I am on my way to Winifredo Lecramberti."

"Mason is up there watching," said Gilray. "The Old Man thinks Herf might make a contact."

"And the Old Man may have something there, Gilray. All right, I'll report when I've seen her."

"Watch out for that dame, Grant. She likes to take her clothes off."

"You're telling me," laughed Grant.

He put down the instrument, got out of bed and went into the bathroom. He bathed, shaved and dressed in twenty minutes, all his movements smooth and effective without wasted energy.

When he rang the bell of the flat she opened the door to him, her eyes bright, her lips smiling a welcome. Grant saw with some relief that she was wearing a polo-necked sweater of green wool and a pair of black jeans, skin tight. The sweater might come off easily, but those jeans would not.

There was a cheerful fire burning in the lounge. The softly shaded lights made it an attractive room, suggesting snug comfort. She said: "This is wonderful, darling Ian." and put her arms about his neck, kissing him. He kissed her in return with enough warmth in it to satisfy her.

She went over to the cabinet and took out a bottle of whisky and two glasses. Grant watched her pour heavy tots in each. He didn't think she would try any tricks, but he was going to be sure. When cigarettes were lighted she sat on the divan, close to him and slipped her hand under his arm.

"Well," said Grant, "what have you to tell me?"

"That you are quite the most wonderful man I've ever met, my big Ian."

"I know. You told me that before. And I think you are quite incredible. Now tell me what I want to know."

"Kiss me first."

He kissed her. She held him tightly, her lips like burning cushions against his own. In the end he had to push her away, gently, but firmly. He had to keep thinking of Jenny. If he didn't, he knew she would have her way with him.

"Eric Siloffski is in London, darling," she said. "I thought you'd want to know that."

"How do you know?"

"He telephoned me. He wants to see me again."

"What did you say to that?"

"I stalled. I wanted to talk to you first. I think he's a Polish Secret Service agent, and high up, too."

"You have evidence?"

"No, only suspicions."

"He was the man with the eagle tattooed on his arm?"

"That's right, like Peter Herf, alias Mikoff."

Grant thought fast.

"Herf?" he said. "I thought you said his name was Heffle."

"So it was when I first met him in Italy. But his real name is Herf. He told me so. Of course, he could have lied. He used the name of Weidmann, too. Does the name mean anything to you?"

"No."

She stared at him. "I think it does, darling."

"Herf, Heffle, Mikoff, Weidmann or any other name, it's still the same man. I think he may come here sometime soon."

He saw the glint of fear in her eyes. It was momentary, but it was real.

"I hope not. I don't want ever to see him again, except as a corpse. He's caused me enough trouble as it is. Why do you say that? I'm sure not to scare me."

"No, to warn you. In confidence I will tell you. He's on the run."

"From the Russians?"

"He may be. But certainly from the police. His drug racket has been exposed. They want him.

"Why do *you* want him, Ian?"

"He may have some papers stolen from the Foreign Office."

"By Morgan Porthy?"

"By someone."

"In the Foreign Office?"

"Yes. Would you have any ideas?"

"No. Not really. Porthy was thick with a man named Hemmer, who is in the Foreign Office. He had a mistress, the wife of a Pole, named Klutz. And he brought a Dutch girl to Porthy's flat, too."

"What was her name?"

"Van something. Van Dansen. I liked her. She was young and gay. Too good for Hemmer. He is a nasty type. I can't imagine he even began to know how to treat a woman decently."

Grant was thinking that both women she had named appeared among Porthy's collection of nudes. And Hemmer was on Bathic's staff, senior to Morgan Porthy, one of the secretaries. Hemmer was being watched, but the Old Man would be very interested in this additional information.

The door bell rang. "Oh, damn," swore Winifredo. "Let it ring. I'm not answering."

"Whoever it is can see the light if he looks through the letter-box."

The bell kept ringing. The caller was not to be denied. Grant said: "Stay here, I'll answer."

"I'm not at home, darling. Get rid of him."

Grant eased the gun in its holster under his left arm-pit. The caller might be Herf. He opened the door with a quick jerk. A tall man, about thirty-five years of age, dressed in a heavy black overcoat and black hat stared at him. There was nothing sinister about the man. He looked a good-natured type. But he was startled.

"Oh," he said in English with a slight accent. "I have made a mistake."

"Whom do you seek?" asked Grant.

"A lady named Lecramberti."

"She lives here."

The man stared at him inquiringly: "Then, may I talk to her?" he asked.

"What name?"

"Eric Siloffski. I telephoned her. She knows I am in London."

Grant made up his mind. "Very well. Come in."

Siloffski hesistated. "I don't want to intrude if . . ."

"You don't intrude."

Siloffski walked into the lounge with Grant close behind him. He saw Winifredo give the Pole a smile, a social smile as artificial as paste diamonds. She held out her hand and he bowed stiffly from the waist as he kissed it. Grant said: "Take off your coat. It is hot in here."

The Pole looked at Winifredo, his expression doubtful. Grant said: "I'm not staying. If you two want to talk I'll be on my way."

"No," she said sharply. "Stay, darling. I have no secrets from you."

Grant hesitated. The advent of the Pole was too much of a coincidence. She had let the name of Peter Herf slip from her tongue in an unguarded moment. Her explanation might be true. It might not. He didn't know. He thought of her history and her reputation. She was about as healthy to trust as a wild cat. She might be taking him for a ride, as she had taken so many men. On the other hand, he ought to know more about this Pole.

Mason was out there on the other side of the road, watching. He could find some excuse to signal him. He turned to her and smiled:

"Do you have secrets between you?"

"No," said Siloffski hastily. "We have no secrets. We are old acquaintances, that is all. I am in London. Naturally I would wish to meet Madame Lecramberti again."

"Naturally," nodded Grant. "Well, take off your coat, or you will be baked. I'll open the window for a few moments, my dear. It is too hot in here."

Grant went over, parted the curtains, and opened the window. He stayed breathing the cold night air. He could see Mason as a shadowy figure across the road by the tall privet hedge. He saw Mason raise his hand in acknowledgement of his signal and closed the window again. When he turned

Siloffski had taken off his overcoat and Winifredo was carrying it to the hall wardrobe. He said: "What will you drink, Mr. Siloffski?"

"Brandy, please."

Grant poured him a brandy and passed the glass to him. Winifredo came back, smiling. "Ah, good, you have given Eric a drink. Eric, I haven't introduced you. How stupid of me. This is Ian, my very dear friend."

"Siloffski bowed with his stiff, military bow from the waist, but did not offer to shake hands. Grant had the impression that he had expected to find her alone. It eased some of the suspicion in his mind.

When they were seated, the Pole in a chair and Grant and Winifredo on the divan, she said, directly: "Well, Eric, to what do I owe the pleasure of this visit?"

"To see you again, of course," he said and tried to smile, but it was no more than a nervous twist of the lips. Grant realized than that the man was scared, but had been holding himself with admirable control.

"I've told you," she said gently, "that I have no secrets from Ian. What you tell us we will treat as confidential. There are no secret police here, Eric. You can trust us."

Siloffski looked towards the door, like a hunted animal about to bolt. He glanced at Grant, sitting poker-faced beside Winifredo, sipping his whisky.

"I did want some information," he admitted. "I thought you might be able to help me."

"All right, Eric," she smiled. "Try me."

The Pole's agitation was genuine, Grant was sure of that. He gulped the brandy and set the empty glass upon the table at his side. Winifredo went over to the mantlepiece, took up a box of cigarettes, opened it and extended it to him. He took one with fumbling fingers. Grant stood up, flicked flame to his lighter, lit the Pole's cigarette and one for her, and himself.

"I have information that two men of the Russian Embassy were drowned very recently, Zidkov and Mikoff. Would you know if that is true?"

Grant wondered how he knew. The information had not been given to the Press, as yet, there had been no inquest.

Winifredo glanced at him, seeking a lead. He said, taking a chance: "Yes, I believe it is. How did you get the information?"

"I saw a small paragraph in a French newspaper."

Grant thought he lied, but he let it pass. Eric Siloffski intrigued him.

"If you really want this information I might be able to help you. Is it important to you?"

"Yes."

"May I ask why?"

Siloffski glanced at Winifredo, uncertain, a man who was afraid to trust anybody, but one desperately needing help.

"I wish I could be sure you——"

"Forget it," snapped Grant. "If you ask us to help you we want to know why. If we don't like what you tell us, all right, we do nothing about it. But Winifredo has had enough of political intrigue. She doesn't want to become involved again, you understand."

"Yes," said Siloffski, very quietly. "I do understand, and I do need help. I must trust you."

"Very well, let's have it." Grant's voice was brisk.

Siloffski rubbed his hands together and gave one swift glance around the room as if fearful of being overheard. When he spoke his voice was not much more than a husky whisper.

"Mikoff is not dead," he said. "I have seen him."

They said nothing, waiting. Their silence seemed to make the Pole more nervous than ever. At last he said, more forcefully:

"Don't you see this is important?"

"It may be to you," shrugged Grant. "And, perhaps, to the Russians, or the British police, but not to us. How can you be so sure the man is alive? After all, it is unlikely that such a mistake could be made."

"That is the very point which worries me. How could such a mistake have been made?"

Grant shrugged again, indifferently: "I suppose it could happen, if someone wanted it that way, especially Russians. Where did you see Mikoff?"

"I was visiting a friend, a Pole exiled in this country. I saw Mikoff leave the house by a side entrance as I came down the road. When I questioned my friend he denied it was Mikoff. I don't understand it."

Grant had a shrewd idea then. Siloffski was running with the hare and hunting with the hounds, a double agent, and he'd got himself in a very nasty tangle.

"Your friend was probably right," said Grant.

"No. I am absolutely sure it was Mikoff. I should know him anywhere, if only by his walk."

"Do I know your friend, Eric?" asked Winifredo, sympathetically, in marked contrast to Grant's offhand manner.

"You know so many people," Siloffski managed a twisted smile. "It is Count Hans von Drackenburg."

"I'm not sure, Eric. I think I do know him. I went to a house in Putney . . . "

Siloffski shook his head. "Von Drackenburg lives outside London, in a village, quite close to where my mother was born. She was English, you know."

"I didn't know," said Winifredo.

"In any case," shrugged Grant, impatiently, "what does it matter? Why should you be scared because Mikoff is alive?"

"Scared?"

"Yes, damn it, you are scared. I don't wish to be offensive, but you are asking our help. What are you, a Polish secret agent, or something?"

"Would you help me if I were?"

Siloffski's voice had a tight, hard sound like an overdrawn wire.

"We might. It would depend on what you wanted."

Siloffski looked down at the floor, crushing the cigarette between his fingers, a man near the end of his tether, unable to make up his mind. Grant said, almost brutally: "It seems to me, Siloffski that you may have been playing a dangerous game. If you have Polish friends exiled in this country you can't be all that loyal to the present Polish government. If you've got a foot in both camps you are asking for big trouble."

The Pole stared at Grant, fearfully, as if he carried the odour of death upon him.

"Who . . . who are you?" he whispered.

"Never mind that," snapped Grant. "If you want help you'd better tell me the truth. Who is Mikoff?"

"I told you, a Russian attached——"

"You know he's not a Russian. You know his real identity. That is why you are so scared."

Siloffski looked like a man who thought he had plumbed the uttermost depths of fear and now finds darker depths still awaiting him. Winifredo got up and poured him another brandy, a very large one. He gulped it, coughing as the spirit caught his throat.

She said, a hand upon his shoulder: "My poor Eric, you *are* suffering from shattered nerves. Is it that Mikoff followed you here?"

"Oh, my God, don't say that! No, no, I'm sure he has not. How could he?"

"Not if he's dead," said Grant grimly. "If he's alive I wouldn't put it past him. Once Mikoff gets on a man's trail you might as well start digging that man's grave. Mikoff never fails."

Siloffski put his head in his hands and rocked himself to and fro, moaning. Winifredo gave Grant a frown. "Is it necessary?" she whispered.

"Yes," nodded Grant.

Winifredo went over and put her arm about Siloffski's neck in a comforting gesture. Grant looked on, thinking hard. He had the Pole on the run. With a little more pressure he'd get the truth. After a couple of minutes he said, sharply:

"Pull yourself together, Siloffski. Maybe we can save you from Mikoff. But we want the truth about yourself, and, remember, nothing but the truth. Who is Mikoff?"

Winifredo came back to sit at Grant's side. Siloffski took his hands from his face. He looked pale, drawn and haggard.

"You are a British Intelligence officer," he said.

"Never mind who I am. All you have to think about is the help I can give you."

"Very well," said Siloffski wearily. "I am as you suggested a Polish agent. I am, or was, a member of an association which seeks to overthrow the present government Inevitably, I suppose, I have fallen foul of both sides. Mikoff is a German-Pole named Peter Herf. The association believes him to be a loyal member. I know differently."

"You mean he is working for the present Polish government?"

"No. He did work for the Russians as an agent in America and West Germany. But really he is a criminal working for himself. He is supposed to be earning money for the association, but none of it has yet been paid over. It all stands in his name in a French bank."

"Have you told Count von Drackenburg this?"

"Yes. He does not believe me. He is a foolish old man. He will not listen. He accused me of being a spy."

"Are you?"

"I tried to shield them until I found it impossible. The Polish security services found out what I was doing. I escaped from France just in time. Now I don't know what to do. If you know so much, tell me, are there any of the Polish agents in England?"

"I wouldn't know. That's not my department. What does this association hope to accomplish?"

"Originally it hoped to restore the old German-Polish aristocratic families to power. The founders were largely Army officers with secret German support. The membership changed a great deal over the years, but it has always been very much anti-Russian."

"Would you consider this association to be a danger to the Polish government?"

"No, I don't think so. But you never know. There is much discontent among all the country folk in Poland, and in the towns. But any uprising would be another Hungary. I joined the security forces to aid the association, but I now realize I have been very foolish. Peter Herf has worked himself into a position of great power in the association. He would sell us out to the Communists without a second thought if they paid him enough."

"Indeed he would," agreed Grant. "What do you know of Stephan Morizov?"

"I know him well. He was a member, but he has taken no active part for years. When he finally settled in London he would have liked to resign. But there is no resignation. Only death frees a man."

Grant nodded: "You've certainly got yourself in a nasty trap, Siloffski. The odds are the Russians will be on your trail, too."

"I know. I fear them more than my own countrymen."

"Where are you staying in London?"

"I only arrived early this morning. I have not booked a room anywhere yet. My luggage is at Victoria railway station."

"So you were hoping that Winifredo would shelter you?"

"Yes."

"You can get rid of that idea. She's had enough trouble without sheltering a potential corpse. You'd better stay the night with me. In the morning we will consider what is best to do for you."

"You are very kind. I . . . I don't deserve it."

"I'll say you do not. But we've got you, so we must do something about it. I don't want Herf to add another murder to his record. What do you know about Zoya Alexandrovna?"

Siloffski shook his head. "I do not know anyone of that name."

"She is a close friend of Peter Herf."

"Perhaps if you described her I might recognize her."

Grant described the girl, very accurately. But still the Pole did not admit he knew her. Grant believed him. There was no reason why he should know her, but it would have been interesting if he had.

"Well," said Grant presently, "if I am to take Siloffski with me I must telephone." He got up and went out to the hall closing the door behind him. He dialled the office and heard Gilray speak.

In a few very brief sentences he explained the situation to him.

"I want two more men up here," he said. "One to relieve Mason. Both to stay all night, and armed. Siloffski thinks he escaped from France, but I can't help feeling he was let go. He's probably got agents trailing him. I'm not so much concerned with his safety as that of the Lecramberti woman."

"Is she all that wonderful?" asked Gilray, and Grant could imagine his twisted grin.

"She's all that useful, if she stays alive," he retorted. "How soon can you get them up?"

"Give me an hour. I'll phone you when they are in position."

Grant went back to the lounge. "There's no hurry," he said. "But I'm going out for a short while."

"Oh, Ian!" exclaimed Winifredo. "Must you?"

"Yes. You give Siloffski another drink and a bite to eat. He looks as if he needs both."

He put on his hat and coat and went down to the street. When he emerged from the building his eyes were alert, but he saw no one loitering. He walked up the hill, crossed at the top and came down on the other side. Mason was there in the deep shadows of the privet hedge. Grant stepped in beside him. He stayed ten minutes talking to Mason, giving him detailed instructions.

"Where's your car?" he asked as he concluded.

"Just round the corner."

"All right. You know what to do. Gilray is sending up two men, probably Todd and Jordan. I want one in and one out."

"That is if nothing happens before you leave with the Pole?"

"Yes."

Grant went back to the flat. Winifredo came out to the hall, closing the door. She said in a whisper: "He's eating in the kitchen. Must you do this, darling?"

"Do what?" asked Grant, kissing her, smiling.

"Take him to your flat?"

"Why not? He has to sleep somewhere, and I'd hate the thought of him sleeping here."

"Because you think he would sleep with me?"

"Because he might bring you big trouble. He didn't escape from France. They let him go. I'll lay long odds he's been trailed ever since."

"Is that why you went out?"

"Yes."

"Did you see anyone?"

"No. But that doesn't mean they aren't there."

"You frighten me, darling."

"Don't worry. I have you covered. Nobody will get at you."

"Oh, Ian, must you leave me? I feel so safe with you. That damned Pole has ruined everything for me. I was so looking forward to having you all to myself. Can't you have an escort for him, if you must put him up at your flat?"

"No, I must take him myself."

She sighed, shaking her head. "It's no use pleading with you, I know."

"Let's get this Herf business over first, my dear. Then we'll both have time to relax. Now, let's go in."

He opened the lounge door and crowded her in before she could get her arms about his neck. He felt sure Siloffski meant nothing to her.

Fifty minutes later the telephone rang. Grant answered. He heard Gilray's voice informing him Todd and Jordan were there.

Siloffski looked at him as he returned to the lounge. Grant said: "All right, we can go."

The brandy had restored some colour to the Pole's cheeks, but it had stimulated the uncertainty and suspicion in his mind.

"Why are you doing this for me?" he asked.

"Because I don't want to see you murdered."

"I may not be in danger."

"No? Very well, get out and find your own bed for the night." Grant's voice was sharp and angry. "But don't come here again. I couldn't care less what happens to you, Siloffski. But I do care what happens to Madame Lecramberti."

He felt her slip her hand under his arm, squeezing affectionately. He hoped he hadn't overdone it.

"Yes, I understand," said Siloffski

humbly. "I am sorry. I will come with you. I am very grateful for your aid."

"So you should be," snapped Winifredo, a vicious note in her voice. "A hell of a lot you thought of me when you came here."

"But, what could I—"

"Forget it," said Grant. "Go on, walk slowly down. I'll catch you up."

Siloffski went out to the hall and began to put on his heavy overcoat. Grant took her in his arms and kissed her, holding her tightly. He felt she had earned it.

He walked down the stairs behind Siloffski and let him step out of the entrance porch before he followed. His car was standing in the drive and he moved towards it, alert and watching. He slid into the driving seat and thrust open the door for the Pole to get in beside him.

In the mirror he saw the black saloon glide out of the side road. Five minutes later he was sure it was following him, but he did nothing to shake it off.

20

ABOUT THE SAME time as Grant was leaving Winifredo Lecramberti's flat, Danny the Dip, elegant, debonair, a credit to his tailor, was sauntering along Piccadilly, humming a popular melody to himself. No one seeing him would have suspected that he had just had a most unpleasant shock which had left him more than a trifle nervous.

True he was not really sure, but near enough certain to be possessed with an urgent desire for flight. He stopped and looked into a shop window displaying winter sports outfits. The big man was still there. Danny was certain now, even though tinted glasses hid the man's eyes.

Danny was a "dip" of the first order. His hands were things of beauty, kept soft and sensitive by the most scrupulous care and daily applications of special oils. His manner was charming and unforced. He radiated good fellowship and honesty. His pleasant, somewhat absented-minded expression gave no hint of the wily, cunning brain, or the audacity of which he was capable. What Danny lacked was physical courage. The thought of being hurt filled him with terror. The sight of blood made him feel sick and faint.

That the man who followed him would beat him to a pulp if he got the opportunity Danny felt certain. He had to elude him somehow. It was while he was making up his mind what to do, that he became aware of another man at his side. He turned his head and recognized him. Danny was not a religious man, but in that moment he felt that this was an Act of God.

"Why, hello, Inspector!" he said, his voice not so smooth as it usually was. "How nice to see you!"

Detective Inspector Trotter gave him a big grin.

"What's the matter Danny boy, you look sort of nervous. Got the stuff on you, eh?"

"Stuff?" exclaimed Danny. "Oh, no, you are quite wrong. You know I've been going straight ever since that last little misfortune."

"Sure, I know," grinned Trotter. "Well, come on, Danny. Take a walk with me."

"Delighted," agreed Danny so readily that Trotter wondered what was on his mind. "Where are we going?"

"Just to have a little chat with Mr. Bellamy. He can't sleep. He wants you to tell him one of your bed-time stories."

A taxi crawled into the kerb. Trotter opened the door and half pushed Danny inside. He gave no order to the driver, who grinned at Danny.

"Ten years, this time, Danny," he said. "You know what the judge told you last time."

"He was prejudiced," retorted Danny. He glanced out of the cab window as it drew away, but he could not see the big man. He sat back against the cushions, vastly relieved, feeling once more at ease. He had nothing to fear from the police. He had not operated this evening and he had nothing compromising in his rooms. He had no idea why he should be picked up in this manner, but he wasn't worrying. He was too glad to have escaped his shadower.

They rode the short distance to the

Yard in silence. Trotter took him by the arm when they alighted and walked into the somewhat bleak H.Q. of the Metropolitan Police.

When he was ushered into Bellamy's room, Danny was smiling blandly. Bellamy gave him a long stare, not unfriendly, rather one of amusement.

"Smart tailor you use, Danny," he said. "He must be worth a fortune to you. Well, sit down. Any confessions to make before we start?"

"Confessions?" Danny raised his eyebrows in surprise. "You know I am going straight now, Mr. Bellamy." There was just a tinge of disapproval which gave point to his courteous tone. Bellamy laughed.

"You're good, Danny. You're very good. Do you feel equal to speaking the truth and nothing but the truth?"

Danny's cunning brain was working fast. He began to have some suspicion of what it might be all about. It was not a happy thought, but the police were better than the big man. At least they wouldn't beat him up.

"You do me an injustice, Mr. Bellamy,"

he said. "I wouldn't lie to the police. You know that."

"That's fine. I don't want to charge you, because I'm not sure you did it. But if I think you are trying to pull a fast one on me, well, you'll get the full treatment, Danny."

"Charge me?" exclaimed Danny. "With what? I've done nothing illegal. Simply because I've been unfortunate—"

"I should charge you with murder, Danny."

Danny's mouth fell open and his eyes blinked in astonishment.

"Murder!" he croaked.

"Murder, Danny, at Woolwich."

The shock hurried Danny into incautious speech.

"But, Mr. Bellamy," he bleated, "the man wasn't killed. He wasn't even hurt much. Damn it, I saw him tonight. He was following me."

"So?" said Bellamy. "Where did you see him?"

"He followed me from my rooms in St. Giles down to Piccadilly. He was right behind me when Mr. Trotter picked me up."

"Are you quite certain, Danny? If you are lying I'll put you away so long that you'll be a white-haired old man before you come out."

"I'm speaking the truth. I tell you I saw him in Piccadilly. I wasn't sure at first. But I know I'm right. He has a small scar on his chin."

Bellamy glanced at Trotter and nodded. Trotter went out, closing the door, Bellamy leaned across the desk, offering the dip a cigarette. He took it with trembling fingers. Bellamy stood up and came around the desk to light it for him. He half sat on the desk looking down at Danny, who regarded him with nervous eyes.

"Now, Danny," he said, "this is a very serious business. I want the full story, and I want it accurate. You're in big trouble. Only the truth will clear you. So don't be a fool. Understand?"

"Yes, Mr. Bellamy. What do you want to know?"

"How you met the man with the scar on his chin."

Danny sucked in a lungful of smoke in an eager, hungry manner. He saw quite clearly that he would have to tell the truth, even if it got him five years. He blew out the smoke with an audible sigh.

"I had been down to see a friend at Plumstead. I was driving back along the lower road towards Charlton. Just past the Woolwich Ferry a man stepped off the pavement. It was very foggy and I hit him. I knocked him down and his head struck the road. I got out and helped him up. He was a bit dazed, but I thought fit to leave. I asked him if he wanted a ride anywhere going my way and he was most abusive. So I drove on."

"What did you lift from him?"

"Nothing but some papers in an envelope. They were in his overcoat pocket."

"Too bad! Where are those papers now?"

Danny made a mistake. He said: "They were no use to me. I destroyed them."

Bellamy shrugged. He went back and sat down.

"I thought it was too much to hope from you. But I did think you'd be sensible enough to realize the spot you are in. So you did kill him."

"No," cried Danny, half rising in his agitation. "All right, I didn't destroy them. I sent them poste restante to Charing Cross Post Office."

"In what name?"

"My own, of course."

Bellamy pressed a bell on his desk. A uniformed constable knocked and opened the door.

"Take him away," ordered Bellamy. "Keep him."

Danny opened his mouth to protest, thought better of it, and walked out with the constable. After all, he had spoken the truth. There were papers at Charing Cross Post Office. As soon as Bellamy got them he would let him go. In any case, he had no thought of returning to his rooms until it was daylight. He didn't want to meet the big man in the dark.

Bellamy took up the telephone.

"Get me the night supervisor at Charing Cross Post Office," he ordered.

While he waited he sat at his desk, thinking. If Danny had spoken the truth it would clear up the case for Colonel Borlaise, but it left the police with a great deal of work still to be done. Until Peter Harf was arrested there would be no rest for Barnard and his men.

His call came through. He explained what he wanted and said he would hold the line. He waited ten minutes before the night supervisor informed him that the envelope was there. So Danny the Dip had spoken the truth!

"It contains stolen documents," said Bellamy. "I have the man here who sent them poste restante. If I send him over with an officer will you let him have the envelope?"

"Couldn't it wait until the morning?"

"If it must, but the matter is very urgent. I am well aware that it is against regulations, but I hope you will stretch a point. If I wait, a murderer may slip through my fingers. I don't want to bother the Home Secretary at this hour, so . . ."

"Very well, if it's like that," agreed the supervisor. "But I must have an official demand from you and I must hand it to the man who sent it."

"Thank you," said Bellamy. "I appreciate your co-operation. The man shall be with you in fifteen minutes accompanied by a uniformed officer."

Bellamy took up a sheet of official notepaper and wrote the order. He pressed a bell for the detective sergeant on duty. When he came he gave him the letter and instructions.

"Take two uniformed constables with you, Martin," he said. "Those documents are very important."

As the sergeant went out, Bellamy reached for the telephone and dialled Ian Grant's number.

21

GRANT DROVE HIS car into the private lock-up at the rear of the block. He went in through the side door, making Siloffski walk ahead of him. His flat was on the first floor. He ignored the lift, walking up the stairs. An ascending lift might serve as a warning. Not that he expected trouble, but he never neglected routine precautions.

He unlocked the door and stood aside for Siloffski to enter, and reached in to switch on the hall light. When he closed the outer door he bolted it. The only other entrance to the flat was by the fire escape at the rear.

"Well," he said, as they went into the lounge, bright and warm after the damp cold of the night, "you should be safe for tonight, at least."

"I am very grateful to you, Mr. Grant. I know what you're thinking of me, and, perhaps, I deserve your condemnation. But I haven't had very much choice.

If Peter Herf had kept out of things I would have remained loyal to the association. But now he is in virtual control I'd be a fool to risk my life any longer helping them. I've done my best to warn them, but they don't believe me."

"So you said. But you've put yourself in a hell of a position. If the British police get hold of you the odds are you will be sent back to Poland."

"I could claim political asylum, couldn't I?"

"I shouldn't count too much on that, Siloffski. Too many people have claimed political asylum who have subsequently been identified as Communist agents."

"You surely don't think that I—"

"I'm not concerned whether you are or not. I just want to make sure you stay alive long enough for Herf to be arrested."

"And if he is, what then happens to me?"

"That will be for my chief to decide. I shall talk to him in the morning. It may be that he will ask you to help us."

"I am prepared to assist you in any

way I can," declared the Pole earnestly.

Grant smiled, rather grimly: "Good! It might solve your problem."

The telephone shrilled. Grant went over and took up the instrument. It was Mason, who said: "You were tailed, Grant. Three gorillas in a black saloon. I'd say they were Russian strong-arm boys. I've got the car number, for what it may be worth."

"Where are they now?"

"They drove away, but I wouldn't guarantee that they went very far. They had a look round the rear of your place first. What do you want me to do? I've got a feeling they'll be back."

"Keep watching. Call me if you see them. Call me in an hour in any case. All right?"

"Sure. It's going to be fun. It's started to rain. Have a nice warm drink on me. So long."

Grant had scarcely put the instrument down before it rang again. He heard Bellamy's voice inquiring for him. "Grant here," he said, feeling the excitement stirring within him.

"I think it possible that I have located

your papers, Grant. I'd like you to come down and identify them."

"Have you contacted Colonel Borlaise?" asked Grant.

"No. I'll do that when I'm sure I have the right documents. Or you can."

"All right, I'll be on my way. Many thanks."

He looked at Siloffski, who was watching him anxiously.

"I have to leave you," he said. "I shall not be away very long. Bolt the door after me. Nothing very much can happen to you in the short time I shall be absent."

"I've been followed here, haven't I?"

"My guess is you've been followed from France. You got away too easily, Siloffski, if you were suspected."

"Is anyone out there now?"

"Only a colleague of mine. Keep all the lights burning. I'll knock three times, like this, when I return." Grant rapped with his knuckles on the table. "Got it?"

"Yes," said Siloffski in a nervous whisper. "But I would feel much safer if I had a pistol."

Grant shook his head. "You don't need a pistol. In any case, I haven't one to spare. So just stay here quietly until I return."

"If they are watching and see you go they may break in. They will know I am here."

Grant stared at him. Maybe it was as well to be sure. He took up the telephone and dialled Bellamy's number. When he was through, he said: "I'd like a patrol car watching my flat while I'm with you. Will you fix it?"

"Yes," agreed Bellamy. "Expecting trouble?"

"You never know. I'll tell you when I see you. Instruct your men to watch out for a colleague of mine named Mason. He's standing out in the rain, poor devil."

"That gives you police cover," Grant said as he put down the instrument. "Help yourself to a drink. Try reading. There are plenty of books in the case."

He found Mason in the doorway, sheltering from the pouring rain. He told him where he was going. Mason said: "Looks like the job may be completed."

"The job will not be completed until we have Herf. For the first time we've really identified the man. We've got him out on a limb. If we don't get him now we never shall."

Grant drove on to Scotland Yard. He was uneasy at leaving the Pole. But Mason was there, and a police car would very soon be on the scene.

A uniformed constable conducted him to the chief superintendent's room. Bellamy was standing by the window looking out upon the Embankment. He turned as Grant came in.

"Sit down, Grant," he said. "I'm waiting for the papers. I hope we've had luck."

While they waited Bellamy told him how Danny the Dip had been picked up and questioned.

"He's an amusing scoundrel, Grant, but he was a very worried man when he discovered Herf had located him.

"I wonder how Herf did that?"

Bellamy shrugged: "He would have remembered Danny. He would know he was a professional pickpocket. All he had to do was make inquiries among the criminal fraternity. It was easy enough."

"Do you think Trotter has any chance of picking him up?"

"We have to try, but I don't think Trotter will have much chance, unless Herf is crazy enough to hang around Danny's rooms, waiting for him to return. The odds are he would conclude Danny has been arrested."

"That leaves him where he started," said Grant.

A knock sounded on the door and Detective Sergeant Martin came in. He laid a long envelope upon the desk and stood waiting. Bellamy pushed the envelope towards Grant.

"You'd better open it," he said.

Grant slit the envelope with a penknife. He was conscious that his fingers were tingly with excitement. But when he drew out the sheets of quarto paper neatly pinned together he knew at once these were not the documents he was seeking.

He spread them out on his knee, turning the sheets rapidly. Every page was written in Russian and from his swift perusal appeared to be a precis of Russian naval strength and distribution of ships and submarines, together with land contacts in foreign countries, particularly the U.S.A. It might be a very important discovery, but it was not what he had expected.

"Well?" demanded Bellamy.

Grant shook his head: "No, not the documents we want."

"What are they then?"

"Something stolen from a Russian Embassy, probably here in London. We shall want them, of course."

Bellamy turned to Sergeant Martin. "Bring that damned crook up here again," he ordered.

Grant continued to look over the papers. He said: "These papers were refolded when they were put in the envelope. They'd been carried in a pocket for some time. I'd say an inside pocket. Danny said he got them from the overcoat pocket, didn't he?"

"Yes."

"Well, it could be possible. But I think he's a liar."

The door opened and Danny the Dip was hustled into the room. Sergeant Martin stood holding him by the arm. Bellamy gave him a cold, hard stare before he said: "Where are the other papers you stole?"

Danny looked astonished: "Other papers? I put all the papers in that envelope and posted them, as I told you."

"When you lifted the papers they were in an envelope?"

"Yes. Very old and dirty. I tore it up."

"What was written on the envelope?"

"Nothing. At least, I didn't notice anything."

"You took those papers from his jacket pocket, Danny. They were not the only things you stole. Come on, I want the truth."

"But, but," stammered Danny, "I didn't take . . . oh, well, yes I did, now I remember—"

"The truth, Danny," snapped Bellamy.

"Oh, well, if you must know, there was a roll of five pound notes, ten of them."

"In his overcoat pocket?"

"Yes, with the envelope."

Bellamy stared at him. Danny returned his stare, his eye's mild and innocent. Bellamy leaned forward, pointing with his forefinger:

"Listen, Danny," he said, slowly, impressively. "If you are lying to me and you are still in possession of other papers stolen from this man I wouldn't give a bad half-crown for your chances. You'll be a dead man before another week is out. So, let's have the truth."

"I have told you the truth, Mr. Bellamy. It's no use trying to frighten me. I can't tell you any more. If what you say is true, lock me up. I'll confess to two dips which maybe you don't know about."

"No. I'm turning you loose. You can go to hell your own way. If you're dead you'll save us a damned lot of trouble. All right, Sergeant. Throw him out."

As he spoke Bellamy made a barely perceptible sign to the detective sergeant.

Danny looked scared.

"I'm confessing to those dips," he almost shouted. "You must arrest me."

"I'm not interested in you, Danny," said Bellamy. "It's the other man I'm after. I can put you away any time I wish. When he's cut your throat I shall have him where I want him, on a murder charge. If I were you I'd stay locked in for the next week. All right, take him, Sergeant. He makes me sick."

Danny opened his mouth to wail a

protest, but the detective sergeant was a big man and hustled him out.

"He was lying," declared Grant as the door closed.

"Some of the time. Not all. What is he concealing? Do you think there really were more documents? Or did he just whip a watch, wallet and, perhaps, a passport. Frankly, he had me guessing."

"He confessed to the five pound notes."

"He did. And that's very odd, Grant. I'll swear he spoke the truth there. I was watching him closely. He found those notes in Herf's overcoat pocket all right. From which I would conclude that Herf was either going to pay someone quickly, within a few minutes, without wanting to take his wallet from his pocket. Or he had just lifted them from somebody and was in too much of a hurry to stop and put them in his wallet."

"The Jap, Haika Haisai, maybe."

"That's my guess."

"By the same reasoning he could have taken these papers from the Jap. That's why they were in his overcoat pocket."

"Yes."

"I can't help feeling, Bellamy that you

255

should have worked on Danny a little longer. He didn't look very brave to me."

Bellamy smiled: "The police don't have your advantages, Grant. Questions can be asked in Parliament about us. We exist. You do not."

"So what do you propose to do now?" demanded Grant, appreciating Bellamy's position, but thinking he could have been more determined to make the man speak the truth. Unless, of course, he had turned the job over to the sergeant.

"Danny will be watched night and day. If there are others papers he may attempt to recover them, because he must think they are important enough to take the risk. But I feel that Herf will strike first. Then we'll have him."

"I hope you are right," said Grant. "I think Colonel Borlaise will wish to question Danny, too."

"If so, I can't stop him, Grant. But you'll put me in a very unpleasant position if you try any rough stuff on Danny."

The telephone on Bellamy's desk rang. Grant saw him frown as he listened. He said: "Hold the line," and looked at him.

"The patrol sergeant reports that he has been unable to contact your colleague, because he is lying unconscious in the yard at the rear."

"So?" whispered Grant and swore beneath his breath. "Tell him to wait. I'm coming over at once."

"I'll send a man with you," said Bellamy, and gave his orders to the patrol sergeant. When he put down the instrument he pressed a bell to summon a messenger.

22

DANNY THE DIP for all his skill and audacity was a superstitious man. As Detective Sergeant Mortlake and Detective Constable Keen walked him into the block of flats in which he resided Danny had seen the white cat cross before them. He had arisen from his bed shortly after noon with the feeling that it was going to be a bad day. Events had proved how right he was. The white cat was the last fatal omen which decided him.

The sergeant opened the door of Danny's flat and pushed him inside. He left him standing in the tiny hall while he searched the rooms, making sure Danny would be alone.

"All right, Danny boy," he said, when he returned. "It's all yours. Take Mr. Bellamy's advice and stay under cover. I haven't time to attend your funeral."

"Thank you, sir," replied Danny. "I know you mean well, but I've had enough trouble for one day. I shall stay here until you advise me that it is safe for me to reappear."

The two detective officers left Danny and went down the stairs. The rain was lashing the pavement as the sergeant went out in a run to the police car, leaving the constable in the passageway. He posted a second constable across the street in a shop doorway and drove around the block to the narrow street at the rear. Here he left another constable.

"You're going to have a wet night, Hawkins," he said. "Keep your eyes open. Danny won't stir out, but the other man may take a chance on going in. There's a car circling the block. Good luck."

Detective Sergeant Mortlake returned to Scotland Yard, very glad he wasn't out in the rain all night.

In his room Danny worked fast. He packed a small suitcase, put out the light and stole soft-footed into the corridor. He knew what the police didn't know, that he could go over the roof to the adjoining building and reach the alley by way of a fire escape.

He had no faith in police protection, or in police motives. He felt quite sure that they would put his life in peril to catch the man they wanted.

The rain hit him in a cold, chilling downpour as he emerged upon the roof, hidden from the street by a balustrade. He groped his way in the darkness across the next roof and put his feet on the iron steps of the fire escape. He descended cautiously to the yard below, crossed it and eased open the double doors. Keeping his back against the wall and moving sideways he reached the cross street where he had a lock-up garage.

His fingers were quivering as he fumbled the key in the lock, opened the door and slipped inside. He dared not risk a light. The noise of the self-starter roared like thunder in his ears. He was letting in the clutch when the car door opened and a man slid in beside him.

"Drive," ordered the man in a harsh voice, heavy with a foreign accent.

Danny recognized that voice. His heart hammered against his ribs and his throat was so dry that he nearly choked. His hands on the wheel were slippery with cold perspiration and he felt suddenly very sick.

"Drive," repeated the voice, "or I'll kill you right now."

Danny brought the car out of the garage in a series of jerks quite unlike his normal smooth driving.

The man was like a black, menacing shadow beside him, faceless, unreal, filling him with superstitious dread. He was too frightened to have any thought of disobeying.

The only sounds were the creek of the windscreen wipers battling with the rain lashing on the glass, the hum of tyres on the wet road and Danny's uneven breathing.

"Make towards Marble Arch," ordered the man.

Danny turned into Oxford Street, so agitated that he shot the traffic lights at red. When he realized what he had done a new hope flashed in his mind. All he had to do was deliberately crash with another car and he would have a chance.

"Don't get ideas and try tricks," said the man. "You would be dead before the car stopped."

Danny felt a hard object poked viciously into his side. He drove on, filled with growing despair. When they reached Marble Arch the man said: "Go down by the park and draw in."

Danny obeyed. For the first time he risked a glance. He should have seen at least the outlines of a face, but all he could see were two eyes which gleamed faintly in the gloom. It occurred to him that the man either wore a black mask, or his face was completely blacked over.

"Where are the papers you stole from me?" demanded the man.

"The . . . the police have them," stammered Danny. "I was picked-up tonight. I was taken to Scotland Yard. The papers were poste restante at Charing Cross Post Office. The police collected them. Then they turned me loose as . . . as a trap for you."

"I see. What were the papers?"

"You should know," Danny found some shred of courage still left. "I couldn't read the stuff."

"There were papers you could read, an official letter for one, and a passport and money."

It was Danny's misfortune that he was

a natural liar. He never spoke the truth when a lie would serve.

"I didn't see any letters. I didn't look at the papers much. I tore up the passport and put it in the fire. I kept the money."

"Very well," said the other. "I had hoped you would be smarter. I am prepared to pay big money for those papers. But if you prefer to speak the truth the hard way, then so much the worse for you. Turn and go back the route you came. I will give you instructions as you drive."

"Where . . .where are we going?" bleated Danny, fearfully.

"To a place where you will tell me the truth."

"But I have told you the truth."

"You have not. I am aware that the police took you tonight. I waited in the expectation that you would be liberated. No doubt you successfully hoodwinked them. But you do not hoodwink me. I give you one last chance, where are the papers?"

Danny made up his mind. It was his only hope.

"In my rooms."

"You lie. I have already searched your room. I cannot waste further time on a fool. Drive."

Danny asked in a husky whisper: "How much will you pay?"

"If you had not lied I would have paid one thousand pounds. Now you will be content with one hundred, or nothing."

"All right," agreed Danny. "The papers are poste restante at a post office."

"Where?"

"Fulham."

"Drive there."

Danny swung away from the kerb and drove on, horribly aware of the man riding at his side. The lash of the rain was a growing irritation to his tortured nerves. The wipers staggered across the glass like weary fingers about to give up, allowing him only a dripping arc of vision which at any time would have made driving difficult. Now he felt that half the time he was driving blind, terrified of a crash lest the monster with him should carry out his threat.

He would have drawn up outside the

post office, but the other snarled savagely at him. He parked the car in a side turning where it was very dark.

"Get out," ordered the man. "And don't try to run. You wouldn't get three yards away."

Danny had scarcely set foot on the ground before the other was beside him. He felt his wrist seized by a gloved hand with the grip of a vice.

"Walk," said the man.

There was a narrow alley beside the building and a yard at the rear. No light showed anywhere. Standing in the darkness with the rain lashing down upon him Danny was trembling with fear and cold. He heard very faintly the clink of metal. He saw the man put what looked like a rubber cup against the glass panel. Then he observed him insert a hand and arm into the hole made in the glass. A few seconds later the door opened.

"Get in and find those papers. You know where to look for them better than I do."

"But there will be people in there," protested Danny. "There are always sorters and . . . and officials on duty."

"Not at this time of night. Go in and get those papers."

"But I'm not a burglar," protested Danny. "I've never broken in anywhere in my life. I am—"

"There's always a first time. This is it. Now is your chance to learn. Take this torch. And hurry."

Danny went in, pointing his wavering torch beam ahead like a defensive weapon. He hated this. It outraged his professional dignity and he had a dreadful sense of impending disaster. He thought of the white cat which had crossed his path and groaned.

It was not a large post office, but one he had used before. He was familiar with the front and main counter, but not with the rear premises. It took him fifteen sweating, trembling minutes to locate the envelope, placed with a number of others in pigeon holes in a tall frame and arranged alphabetically. He put the envelope in his pocket and turned to flee.

It was then that idea flashed into his troubled mind. He did not for one moment expect to be paid the £100 which had been promised for the job. He thought of the other's pistol and all its sinister possibilities. Probably it was the pistol which made up his mind for him.

He slipped under the counter flap and stole softly to the public telephone booths. With quivering fingers he dialled 999 as silently as possible, perspiration dripping in his eyes with fear and impatience. He was opening his mouth to call "Police" when the door opened behind him. A silencer-fitted pistol coughed once. Danny gave a strangled scream of agony as a soft-nosed bullet ploughed through his back. The instrument fell from nerveless fingers and clattered against the wall as it swung. Danny's knees went and he slid down, propped grotesquely in the angle of the two walls.

The man leaned in, took the envelope from his pocket, picked up the torch, snapped it off, laughed, and vanished in the darkness.

When the police found Danny he was still conscious. He lived just long enough to gasp out his story.

23

"I'M NOT BLAMING you, Grant," said Colonel Borlaise. "You acted correctly. If anyone is to blame it's the police, or Mason. He's still unconscious, so I haven't got his story. The only thing I'm sure of is that Herf has beaten us, for the time being. Bellamy should have known better than to turn that damned pickpocket loose. Having turned him loose he should have made sure he could be kept under observation. The police ought to have known about the exit over the rooftops."

Grant said nothing. The Old Man was steamed up, as well he might be. Borlaise struck a match and lit his pipe, drawing heavily until the tobacco was ignited to his satisfaction.

"Either the Poles or the Russians have got Siloffski. They will make him talk."

"He doesn't know anything too vital, sir."

"He knows enough to make it damned awkward for us, Grant. The way they battered Mason shows the lengths to which they are prepared to go. One thing they will now know is that Herf is alive."

"Have you located Count von Drackenburg, sir?"

"Yes. He lives near Sevenoaks, in Kent. He's known as plain Mr. Drake, a retired South African. I have him covered."

"And Zoya Alexandrovna? The last I heard of her she was still in the Russian Embassy."

"She's home again. They didn't keep her long. I doubt if they put her through it. She may have had the sense to confess. On the other hand, they could have let her go, hoping she may try and contact Herf secretly. She will be shadowed wherever she goes, of course."

"With our people and the Russians she's going to have quite a procession behind her," smiled Grant. "But I can't really see Herf burdening himself with a woman if he means to escape from England."

"She could well be an important link in his escape plans. But it's no use speculating. Herf has made mugs of us, and the police. We've got to get him before the Russians."

"Somewhere he must dump the stolen car. That may give us a lead. And there's still the possibility of the advert in the *Telegraph*."

"That could be our best bet, Grant. That and Lecramberti."

"I'll lay odds she wouldn't help him, sir."

"You may be right. But I'm not trusting her. Neither will the Russians after what Siloffski will have told them. Von Drackenburg is probably regarded by them as their best lead to Herf. But I'm pretty sure they will contact Madame Lecramberti, too. It is possible that Siloffski may have information about her that will enable them to turn the screw. However, that doesn't worry me very much."

The telephone rang. Borlaise answered. Grant heard him say. "Thank you, Bellamy. Yes, probably within walking distance. Must we have the county police? Very well, I leave it to you. Many thanks. Yes, I'll do that."

Borlaise put down the instrument on its cradle. He looked at Grant. "Danver's car has been found abandoned at Otford railway station."

"Within walking distance of Draken-burg's house?"

"Yes. It may be a clever ruse, or he may have parked it there to use again. But I think Herf went to Drackenburg. He could have made it across country in less than an hour. He must still suppose that Drackenburg is free from suspicion."

"In that case there will be no advert in the newspaper," said Grant.

"No. Herf recovered the stolen documents quicker than he had anticipated. Now he's probably all set to bolt from the country."

"If Herf went to Drackenburg our men would have seen him and reported," said Grant.

Borlaise shrugged. "The house is pretty isolated, with extensive woodlands at the rear. If Herf knows the place he wouldn't have much difficulty in getting in un-observed. It was a black night, Grant, pouring with rain. A hell of a night to be watching."

"So what do we do now? Raid the place and hope for the best?"

"Bellamy, in co-operation with the Kent County Police, is having the house surrounded. Then he'll move in. If Herf is there he will be trapped."

"Are you going to be there, sir?"

"Yes."

The telephone rang again. Borlaise answered. He said. "Thank you, Peters. I'll send additional cover."

As he dropped the telephone on its cradle he said to Grant: "Zoya Alexandrovna left her house this morning in a taxi and drove to the Hotel Villa Rosina in Knightsbridge. She's still there, Room 37, second floor. Peters is watching. So are a couple of Russian security officers. Jenny wanted some field work. She can have it. Take the cab. It may be a job for a woman. Send Jenny in. You stay with the cab. The odds are you'll have to follow. Watch out for disguise. That's what I think she will attempt. Unless she's working with the Russians. But I think it unlikely. She appears to be too involved with Herf. They will probably attempt to bolt together."

"She will guess the Russians have tailed her, sir."

"That's why I think she will leave the hotel in disguise."

Grant went out to Jenny. He said: "Come on, we have a job to do together. And it's urgent. Meet me at the garage."

Jenny's eyes lit up. "I can do with a break. What do I need, smart coat or mackintosh?"

"Reversible coat and hat. It may be a shadowing job."

Grant went down to the garage. He put on a chauffeur's peaked cap and shabby old mackintosh. He started up the engine of the taxi cab, a deceptive vehicle, capable of high speed. Jenny came down in a dark green coat and small hat of the same colour. Grant explained briefly what she had to do and Jenny got in the cab.

A hundred yards from the hotel entrance he drew in, keeping the flag down.

"Good luck," he whispered as Jenny paused a moment beside him before she walked on to the hotel. Grant drifted slowly along behind her and stopped.

Jenny was walking towards the lift when she observed the man come into the hotel at a brisk pace, carrying a suitcase. She recognized him, Gordon Hemmer, one of Sir George Bathic's secretaries, senior to the late Morgan Porthy, a man already under suspicion. She felt the thrill of eager anticipation ripple in her veins. Something important was about to happen.

Hemmer ignored the lift and mounted the stairs. Jenny moved over swiftly and entered the lift. It was self-operated. She arrived at the second floor just in time to see Hemmer entering a room at the far end of the corridor at the head of the stairs. She made a swift count of the rooms. Hemmer had gone into Room Number 37.

Jenny walked along the corridor. She paused before the room door, but she could not hear any voices. She went on down the stairs to the public telephone just outside the lounge door. When she got through to her uncle and reported, he said:

"Nice work, Jenny. I'm not surprised. It had to be somebody like that. Watch out for male attire. Is the opposition there?"

"I haven't spotted it yet."

"It will be. Forget it. Warn Peters."

"I can see him in the lounge,"

said Jenny. "How far do we follow?"

"All the way. If they make for a port, you know what to do. In any case, I'll have that covered. Good luck."

Peters did not look at her when she sat in the chair next to him. Opening her handbag Jenny took out mirror and lipstick. As she pretended to work on her lips, she said:

"Cover the side entrance. Gordon Hemmer has gone up carrying a suitcase. The Old Man suggested escape in male attire. Ian Grant is out front in the cab. Where are the Russians?"

"A man and a woman, both in black. The woman has a grey feather in her hat. They're seated in the vestibule. I'll fox them if they try to follow."

Peters glanced at his wrist watch, yawned, folded his newspaper and rose to walk out with a lazy step as if he were very bored and tired. He walked past the man and woman in black. He saw Grant and the cab and went over.

"Sorry, sir," said Grant loudly. "Cab's engaged."

Peters gave him the information as he talked. Then he shrugged and sauntered away towards the side entrance to the hotel.

Twenty minutes later Jenny saw Gordon Hemmer come down the stairs accompanied by a smart young pilot officer of the R.A.F. Jenny could scarcely believe her eyes. No one would have suspected that the officer was a girl. She watched them walk past the man and woman in black. In the entrance they paused. The uniformed doorman went out to flag a taxi for them.

Jenny waited until the taxi drew up. Then she walked out.

"There they are, Ian," she said as she got in. "She makes a handsome man, doesn't she?"

Peters walked past them, shouting to another taxi just turning the corner. The first taxi bearing Hemmer and Zoya moved off. Grant followed.

"Victoria," he said to Jenny. "Catching the boat train for a certainty."

Grant proved to be right. Hemmer and Zoya alighted at the station. Grant drew in as the other cab was moving out. Right behind him came Peters in his taxi. Jenny got out and followed.

Grant slipped off his mackintosh and chauffeur's cap, took up a light-weight coat from the seat and slung it over his arm. Peters sauntered up.

"She fooled the Ruskies," he said. "Looks like Dover for you. What do I do?"

"Drive the cab back to the garage and let the Old Man know what's happening. So long, chum."

"Good killing," grinned Peters. "Mind she doesn't scratch."

Grant saw them by the left luggage office. Hemmer was having a black tin uniform trunk and two large suit-cases loaded on to a trolly. The trunk bore the name, "P/O. G. D. Layton, R.A.F." in white letters. Grant watched as the trolly was wheeled across to the boat train platform. He thought Zoya made a wonderful young man, very smart in the uniform. There was nothing feminine about her walk. Her whole movements were those of a man.

He thought of her as he had first seen her in Porthy's flat, the lithe, feline grace which had seemed to him so wholly feminine then. Her style, the way she wore her clothes, her immaculate white gloves on slender, beautiful hands, everything about her was womanly. Yet now she looked every inch a young man. He found it quite remarkable.

Jenny came to his side. She said: "Get the tickets, darling. Wait for me here. I'd better make the change before we go on to the platform."

She was waiting for him when he returned with two first class tickets for Dover. She had reversed the coat and hat. She was now wearing a tawny-coloured coat and hat to match and of a different shape. A blue scarf about her neck completed the transformation. Grant thought the colours suited her.

As they walked along the train they saw Hemmer and Zoya in a first-class compartment, Hemmer looked like a man suffering from acute nervous strain. It wouldn't take too much pressure to break him. Grant thought the future for Hemmer would not be happy. Zoya, on the other hand, was smiling as if she were enjoying herself. There wouldn't be much future for her either.

"The stage missed a fine actress in Zoya Alexandrovna," said Jenny. "A woman usually gives herself away from the back view. But not Zoya. She'd have deceived me, Ian."

"Me, too."

"You said you found something repellant about her."

"Yes, but I'm damned if I know what it is. Unless it's an evil mind behind all that beauty. She can look very vicious. Here we are, let's get in here."

Grant stood on the platform until the train was starting. He didn't want Hemmer and Zoya to pull a fast one and slip away. That was how Paul Fergus had dodged his shadower, and old trick which had worked successfully.

Twice on the journey Jenny and Grant made separate patrols along the corridor. Hemmer and Zoya were still there. At Dover they waited until they saw them alight and walk towards the luggage van. It was then that they observed the two men move out of the crowd and converge on them. Grant recognized Detective Inspector Tom Norton of the C.I.D.

"Come on, Jenny," said Grant. "We'd better be near."

Grant thought the C.I.D. would have

taken adequate precautions, but he was risking nothing. As they moved in he heard Norton say, very politely:

"You are wanted in the office, Mr. Hemmer. And you, too, sir."

Grant saw the fear flame in Hemmer's eyes. He glanced wildly around, like an animal caught in a trap. Norton's colleague crowded behind Zoya Alexandrovna. Another burly man emerged from among the crowd and joined him.

Hemmer said in a high-pitched, nervous voice: "What's all this about? I'm on holiday."

"I must ask you to come, sir." Norton's voice had lost some of its politeness. The sharp edge of authority had crept in. The two detective constables began to crowd Zoya, forcing her to move.

Grant followed behind them as they went into the offices of the Port Authority, where the C.I.D. had rooms. Norton recognized him. He said: "Well, there they are, Mr. Grant. I'm having their luggage brought in. I'm not too clear what the charge is going to be. My instructions were simply to detain them."

"You can charge the woman with breaking and entering, wearing illegally the uniform of the armed forces and travelling on a false passport. Hemmer as an accomplice. That'll do to take them back to London. I'll search the luggage, too. Maybe that will throw up something meaty."

"Do you want to appear?"

"Yes. After you have searched them. I'll run through the luggage in the meantime."

Detective Inspector Norton went in. Hemmer and Zoya were both smoking cigarettes. Hemmer looked pale and haggard, but Zoya gave him a contemptuous smile. Norton didn't like that smile. It made him feel uneasy. He said: "I have to detain you both. I have to warn you that anything you say may be taken down and used in evidence. You, Zoya Alexandrovna are charged with three offences, breaking and entering, wearing illegally the uniform of the armed forces and travelling on a false passport. You, Gordon Hemmer are charged with being an accomplice. You will both be searched."

"Damn it," protested Hemmer, "this is an outrage. All three charges are nonsense. This is Pilot Officer Layton, attached to the Foreign Office. Damn you, ring the Foreign Office and confirm it before you make ridiculous charges."

"I have my instructions," retorted Norton. "A woman officer will search you, madame. Please step into that room."

"If you think I am going to permit a woman to search me, you are very much mistaken," declared Zoya, still smiling.

"Don't be a fool, Inspector," snarled Hemmer. "Your information is sheer rubbish. Pilot Officer Layton is not a woman."

Norton was shaken. He sensed that something had gone wrong. But he had had definite instructions.

"Very well," he said, "step in. If you want a man to search you, you can have a man. Both of you, go on."

The uniform trunk, and two suit-cases were wheeled in. All were locked. Grant used his keys and opened them. Jenny began on one suit-case, Grant on the other. Jenny's case revealed nothing but Hemmer's clothes. She searched for secret compartments but found none.

Grant's case was full of female attire, nearly all of it new and unworn, elegant and expensive. In a plastic bag containing toilet requisites he discovered the long tube of tooth paste. A slight crease at the base of the tube caused him to take out his knife and slit it along its length. As he had anticipated the tube contained micro-film, three rolls. Further search revealed nothing more. The uniform case had a mixed assortment of male and female attire, but no secret container. With the clothes were two Luger pistols, but no ammunition.

"Well, that's the lot," he said straightening up. "Zoya evidently was going to return to feminine attire. But there is a complete outfit of male attire here, too. I have a feeling that we've been lucky to nobble the lady so soon."

Detective Inspector Norton came into the room. He looked rather grim.

"Mr. Grant," he said, "there has been some mistake. That's a young man, not a woman at all."

Grant stared at him. He was thinking of the curious sense of revulsion he had felt for Zoya Alexandrovna.

"What the hell have I been using for brains all this time!" he exclaimed.

Jenny laughed: "So that was it! I half guessed the truth when I saw him walking across Victoria Station."

"Hemmer was known to be another Paul Fergus," said Grant. "Maybe Morgan Porthy was, too, a damned bunch of queers. Well, it makes no difference, Norton. You'll have to charge him again, as Pilot Officer Layton."

24

THE MIST WAS hanging over the valley and only the chimneys of the old house on the edge of the woods were visible from the road. Bellamy from his point of observation under the high surrounding wall saw the large black saloon car turn into the drive. As far as he could determine there were two other persons beside the driver, seated in the rear. The car went down into the dip and disappeared in the mist.

Detective Inspector Trotter, waiting with Bellamy, said: "That'll be the Russians Colonel Borlaise is expecting. How long are you going to give 'em, sir?"

"Borlaise is over there under the haystack. Go and ask him when he wants us to move in."

Trotter hurried away. Bellamy lit a cigarette, thinking that they could have done without the mist. It would be lying as thick as fog in the woods. With a man like Herf who had proved himself so elusive anything could happen.

He saw Trotter returning and went to meet him.

"The Colonel says move in now. If we wait those Russians may be up to a bit of no good with Drackenburg. He says the third man in the car is Siloffski."

"All right," said Bellamy. "Contact Superintendent Barnard and the County boys. I'll go on slowly with Colonel Borlaise."

Borlaise was standing by the haystack when Bellamy came up to him. "I have given the order, Colonel," he said. "I suggest we move in."

"This damned mist!" complained Borlaise. "I hope you've got the back area well covered. A man wouldn't have to be very smart to dodge a regiment among those trees."

"There are thirty men there, sir. Most of them know the area well. They should be adequate."

"They should be," said Borlaise, as if he doubted it.

Keeping to the turf bordering the drive they walked towards the house. As they ascended from the dip more of the place became visible until they were able to see the front porch. Parked before it was the saloon car. By the bonnet a man in a dark overcoat and black hat was standing, looking towards the house.

"Hold it," said Borlaise. "If we go any nearer we shall be seen."

They halted, waiting for the county police to close in, the main force working in from the woods. At that moment the tall french windows above the terrace flew open with a violence that shattered the glass. A man came out as if he had been shot from a cannon, hurled himself over the balustrade with a reckless urgency eloquent of sheer terror, fell in a flower bed, rose swiftly and began to run towards the drive.

The man waiting by the car whipped a hand in and out of his overcoat pocket, raised it and fired. The report of the pistol came to them clearly, like a sharp crack. The fugitive lurched sideways, took a few staggering steps and fell on his face. The other man walked over, without haste and kicked him in the head.

Bellamy began to run. Behind him he heard the pounding boots of the constabulary. Trotter came out of the drifting mist, running very fast for such a heavy man.

Another figure appeared at the french windows, shouted a warning, vaulted the balustrade and ran towards his companion, who was hauling the fugitive from the ground. He was recovering consciousness and he began to struggle, but together they bundled him into the car, slammed the rear door and while one slid into the driving seat the other ran round the car and got in beside him. Bellamy guessed the prisoner was Siloffski, who, doubtless, had been brought here against his will, probably to try and persuade Drackenburg to co-operate. Siloffski had seen a chance to escape and had risked it, knowing the danger.

The car churned up the gravel as it made too sharp a turn, heading down the drive towards the road. Bellamy saw Trotter check stoop, and pick up a large stone. As the car came on, rapidly gathering speed, Trotter stood in its path until the last split second, hurled the stone at the windscreen and jumped clear.

The glass fractured in a thick, opaque film, blinding the driver's vision, but held to the frame. The car swerved, skidded, and mounted the grass, ploughing across the soft turf, spongy with the recent rains.

Colonel Borlaise drew a .38 pistol and, running towards the car, fired at the petrol tank. At his third bullet a sheet of flame shot up, followed by a loud whoof as the fuel ignited.

Bellamy saw the two men leap out and run towards the drive. He yelled a warning to the constables and dashed towards the blazing car. The rear door opened and Siloffski fell out, his clothes alight. Bellamy dragged him clear and beat out the flames.

Siloffski gasped: "Russian agents."

"Is Mikoff in the house?" demanded Bellamy, but Siloffski had passed out.

From the mist came the sound of shooting. Borlaise had gone in pursuit of the Russian agents. Two constables of the Kent County Police came across the grass to Bellamy when he hailed them.

"Get this man under cover," he ordered. "One of you stay with him. He's burned and shot in the leg. Do what you can for him."

"There's an ambulance standing by, sir."

"All right, take him there. But the ambulance must wait. We may have other casualties."

"What about the car, sir?"

"Let it burn."

Bellamy ran across the lawns to the house. He could see Trotter at the open french windows and Barnard hastening up the steps to join him. Uniformed constables were strung out below the balcony, covering the front. If Herf was in the house he stood a very slender chance of escaping. But Bellamy had a nasty suspicion that Herf wasn't there and they were wasting their time.

When he stepped into the lounge he saw Trotter lifting an elderly man from the floor to prop him in an armchair. The old man's face was deathly pale and he was barely conscious. His left eye was bruised and closed. His nose was dripping blood over his mouth and chin.

Barnard turned when he saw Bellamy. He said: "He's taken a bashing, but it doesn't look too serious. All right, Trotter, leave him. He'll recover."

A sergeant and three uniformed con-stables came in by the hall door.

"Nothing doing yet, sir," reported the sergeant.

Barnard snapped orders and went out with them. Trotter glanced at Bellamy and said, quietly: "Looks like the old man is Count von Drackenburg, sir. He didn't talk fast enough for the strong-arm boys, so they gave him the works."

From the rear of the building police whistles sounded. Bellamy said: "Someone bolting for the woods. Go and see what's happening."

As Trotter hurried out, Bellamy looked down at the battered old man, feebly groaning in the chair. He felt quite sorry for him. Drackenburg's right eye opened and he blinked up painfully. For a few moments he didn't appear to be aware of Bellamy's presence. Then the eye opened wider in sudden fear as he tried to rise.

Bellamy pushed him down, gently.

"I am a police officer," he said. "There is no need to be afraid, Count von Drack-enburg."

The old man closed his eye and sank

back in the chair, breathing heavily. His hand on the chair arm was trembling.

Bellamy went over to the cabinet in the corner, opened it and searched among an assortment of bottles for brandy. He poured a stiff tot and brought it back, holding the glass to Drackenburg's lips.

"Drink," he said. "You'll feel stronger."

Drackenburg sipped gratefully and some faint tinge of colour returned to his cheeks.

"Have you caught them?" he asked in a dry whisper.

"They will not get far. Where is Peter Herf?"

"Not here."

"But he's been here."

"Yes, early this morning. He's stolen my car. My servant, Kellmann will tell you."

"Where has he gone?"

"I don't know. I think he will leave England."

A step sounded outside and Colonel Borlaise walked in.

"Count von Drackenburg states that Herf came here early this morning, stole a car and left again. He does not know where Herf has gone," Bellamy informed him.

"No?" said Borlaise. "Your men are chasing a man who has escaped into the woods."

"Probably the servant. What's happened to the two Russians?"

"Both under arrest. Well, if you like you can leave Count von Drackenburg to me."

"Very well," nodded Bellamy.

He walked out by the hall door. He hoped Borlaise wouldn't be too rough. He thought the old man had had enough for one day.

25

GRANT AND JENNY returned by train, leaving Hemmer and the bogus pilot officer to be brought to London by police car.

"I wonder what's happened at Sevenoaks," said Grant as they settled into a first-class compartment, which they had to themselves. "I can't really imagine that Herf would have laid up there. He couldn't be sure that Count von Drackenburg wasn't being watched."

"He may have taken the chance," said Jenny. "But my money is on Winifredo Lecramberti."

"I'm pretty certain she is genuine in her fear of him."

"So she may be. That's all the more reason she will obey him if he calls on her for aid."

"I see. So that's how you make a woman obey you!" smiled Grant. "I must remember."

"Would you like me to poke you in the eye?"

"I'd rather you kissed me."

She looked at him smiling, her lips full of invitation. Grant kissed her, a long, lingering kiss.

"We're behaving like a couple of juveniles," he said, as he slipped his arm about her waist and drew her to him.

"I like it," declared Jenny. "It's a nice change from work. I hope they've caught Herf."

"So do I. If they have, I shall ask you to marry me."

"What's wrong with now?"

Grant looked at her, saw the dancing devils in her lovely eyes and kissed her again.

"Will you marry me?" he asked.

"What's uncle going to say?"

"Yes."

"Well, that settles it, yes, darling, I love you and I want to marry you. When?"

"Just as soon as we can get leave."

"Where shall we honeymoon?"

"On an island with sandy beaches, sunshine and warm seas. Not many people and none who needs watching. I suggest the Isles of Hyeres."

"That's a nudist colony, isn't it?"

"Only one of the islands."

"It sounds wonderful."

"It is. You'll love it."

They sat together, relaxed and contented, two people who lived so often under great nervous tension and narrow margins of safety, for a brief while able to forget the dangers of their profession.

It was not until they were nearing London that Grant referred to Herf again.

"Now that Herf appears to have recovered the documents lifted from him by Danny the Dip, I think he will attempt to get out of the country as soon as possible."

"Yes," agreed Jenny. "I'm wondering if it would have been better to let that pair go to France, because it is probable they planned to meet Herf there. If he's got a motor-boat or yacht laid on for him somewhere it would be easy enough to escape to France."

"In that case, they would all have gone together, I think. But Hemmer is poor stuff. He's in a highly nervous condition. It'll take very little pressure to break him down. Once the Old Man gets working on him he'll talk fast. The other will not."

Jenny nodded. "No wonder you found

the creature so repulsive. That kind has me baffled I cannot understand them. They must be freaks of Nature."

"Some, maybe, but not all. I still can't think of him as any other than Zoya Alexandrovna. I feel pretty sure Herf is not one of the same breed. But he may be. They're a vicious crowd. It will be interesting to discover Pilot Officer Layton's real identity. The name rings a bell somewhere."

"They must have planned this flight well in advance, Ian."

"Like Burgess and McLean. Perhaps they were going to pull the same trick."

"And join Herf somewhere in England? They wouldn't have left the films in the luggage in that case. Unless, of course, they had made arrangements for the luggage to be collected in Calais. I hope Peters was right and the Russians were fooled. I can't help feeling their system would have been better than that. If they had agents at Dover they know of the arrests."

"In which case Winifredo Lecramberti will come in for attention."

"Yes."

"One thing seems sure in all this mess, Herf's plans have been seriously disrupted and he's on the run, being forced to improvise as best he can. I hope we've closed all the bolt holes."

When they reached Victoria they separated. Grant went into a public telephone booth and got on to H.Q. Gilray answered him.

"The Old Man is still at Sevenoaks," he said. "He telephoned ordering an additional man to be put on to Lecramberti. I sent Mallory. There's nothing you or Jenny can do. Take a rest. If anything blows up I'll telephone you at your flat. O.K.?"

Grant said it was. Very briefly he told Gilray what had happened at Dover.

"I know," said Gilray. "I've had the Yard on to me. What a revelation! Dear Zoya! An absolute Queen! Oh, boy how he had us fooled! Hemmer was due for the chop, anyway. So long."

Grant came out of Victoria Station and crossed the road, walking up Victoria Street towards Westminster. When he reached the Abbey he stopped, waiting. Jenny joined him five minutes later.

"All right," she said. "No one on your tail."

Grant flagged a taxi and gave the address of his flat. He was inserting the key in the lock when he heard the telephone ringing. He hurried into the lounge. Winifredo Lecramberti's voice came over the wire. It sounded agitated.

"Thank God you're there at last. I've been ringing this past hour."

"Take it easy," he said gently. "What's the trouble?"

"Peter Herf telephoned me. He demands that I bring my car to meet him near Dartford, in Kent. If I don't, he threatens to come and get me. What must I do, Ian darling? I'm scared. You know what that man is like. He'll do what he threatens."

"When must you meet him?"

"At five o'clock. I can't delay any longer if I'm going."

"Tell me exactly where you have to meet him."

"There's a mental hospital somewhere on the heath outside Dartford. I have to drive up and down the road along the wall."

"Do you know the area?"

"No, of course not. I don't even know where the damned place is. I'll have to look up the map."

Grant gave her brief but plain instructions how to reach Dartford Heath. He said: "Don't be scared. You'll be well covered."

"Herf knows you have men watching this flat," she told him. "He'll be expecting someone trailing me."

"That's a chance we have to take. We may fail, but no harm will come to you. What's his idea would you say?"

"He's going to make me drive him somewhere."

"Did he say so?"

"No, but that's my guess."

"And mine. All right, go ahead. I think you are a very brave woman."

"So do I. You won't believe this, but I'm doing it for you, Ian darling. I expect you to be nice to me if we pull this off."

"We will, Win. We will. Good-bye."

Grant put down the telephone. Jenny was watching him with just the shadow of a frown on her face.

"Did you have to be so sweet to her?" she demanded.

Grant laughed. "Jealous?"

"Of course not. What was that all about? She has to meet Herf?"

"Yes, at five o'clock on Dartford Heath. We'll have to handle this ourselves. Too late now to get police co-operation. Get on to Gilray and tell him what I'm doing."

"*We* are doing. I'm coming too."

Grant smiled. "I guessed that, but I'd rather you did not. It could be nasty, Jenny."

"I know," she nodded, taking up the phone and beginning to dial.

Grant went down to the garage and got out his car. Jenny joined him a few minutes later. As she slid into the seat beside him she said: "Gilray will get in touch with uncle by radio."

"Good! But, you know, I haven't much faith in this adventure."

"Why not?"

"It's not Herf's style."

"Well, you said he was being forced to improvise. He has to take chances he wouldn't have done. Perhaps he knows Hemmer has failed him. I wonder what those microfilms will show."

"Photographs of secret documents.

Hemmer is due for a very long stretch in prison. How Bathic ever came to have such a man for his secretary is beyond my understanding. Bathic must be more bone-headed than we suspected."

"Old school tie, Ian. Hemmer must have been crazy to ask for one of our people as an escort."

"He did it to cover himself and Porthy. He could pass the buck to us for failure. I feel certain it was intended that Herf would get away with those documents the same night, before the hue and cry was raised for him. Danny the Dip put paid to that."

"A sheer accident."

Grant nodded: "Yes, something the most careful planning can never eliminate. Herf had murdered three people who could betray him and was all set to go, probably with Zoya accompanying him. But of all the people who could have knocked him down in the fog it had to be a skilled pickpocket. Too bad for Herf."

"Why did Weidmann hang out in such uncomfortable conditions at Woolwich?" asked Jenny. "He could surely have lived in an hotel."

"To be near the docks, working with the Jap in the drug racket, collecting the stuff from seamen. That house was ideally situated for the job. It's as dark as the pit along that river embankment at night. I doubt if he knew Herf's real purpose. Weidmann was just a crook and nothing more. He wasn't the sort to get himself involved in international espionage if he had any choice."

Grant drove through South-east London to Blackheath Hill, across the heath, taking the Rochester road. He passed through the village of Bexley and up the hill to the mental hospital on the edge of Dartford Heath.

Rain was falling in misty drizzle, a cold, grey curtain over the gorse and heather and stunted trees. On their right lay the extensive grounds of the hospital behind a high wall. Grant drove straight on until he was able to pull in to a bay among the trees flanking the road.

"I'm going back and patrol the road under cover," he said. "Keep driving, circling round."

"Are you going to recognize Lecramberti's car?"

"Yes. It's a grey and blue Sunbeam, with a big, yellow fog light. She will probably pull in somewhere like this and wait."

"Be careful, Ian," whispered Jenny, as he got out and she slid over into his place behind the wheel.

Grant moved in among the stunted trees, dripping with moisture, cold and clammy. He eased the Luger in the holster under his left arm-pit and wondered vaguely if he would have to use it. He was trying to assess the possibilities, but he had an uneasy suspicion that Herf had pulled a fast one on them, knowing that Winifredo Lecramberti was being watched, not trusting her, guessing that she would inform against him, drawing off the watch to concentrate on his capture at this place while he carried out his plans elsewhere.

He glanced at his wrist-watch, four thirty-five, and already dark enough for anything to happen swiftly and unseen. Why did Herf want another car when he had Count von Drackenburg's car? Maybe he had anticipated that the police would have been looking for it. The odds were that Herf had a boat available somewhere, probably along the Suffolk or Norfolk coasts.

Grant moved through the trees, slowly, alert, because if Herf was here this is what he would be doing, too, might even be stalking him at this very moment. It was an odd, eerie sensation. Grant shrugged it off. That was not a safe way to be thinking.

Cars passed on the road at irregular intervals, their lights half obscured in the thick, misty rain. A few people went past on bicycles or on foot, staff from the hospital probably. He wondered what they would think if they could know what was happening. Most of them, he thought, would be excited and thrilled.

At five minutes past five o'clock a car came along the road, driving slowly. He recognized the Sunbeam. The car went on and drew in at the same spot as he had done. It was then that he saw the motorcyclist stop in the shadows of the trees.

Grant edged towards him, very cautiously. Despite the goggles and crash helmet he recognized Bill Todd, one of the men who had been detailed to watch Winifredo Lecramberti. He called softly:

"Todd, this is Grant." Then he stepped closer. "Jenny is circling in my car. Are you alone?"

"No," said Todd. "Martin and McLellan are back there in the taxi."

"I'm working down towards Lecramberti," said Grant.

He moved away, hastening through the trees towards the car. When he reached it he could see her at the wheel, smoking a cigarette. She didn't look agitated or nervous, although he knew she must be.

Jenny came round again and passed. He wondered if she had seen the taxi. Jenny came round the second time, ten minutes later. He thought she was doing it too often, but he had no means of warning her.

At five-thirty Winifredo Lecramberti let in the clutch and drove on. Grant saw Todd as he passed, following. Three minutes later the scream of tortured brakes and the crash of two cars in violent collision came out of the misty darkness.

Grant waited under cover of the dripping trees, feeling sick with apprehension lest one of those cars should have had Jenny driving. Then he saw his car, coasting slowly along the road. She drew into the bay, stopped, and got out. Grant was at her side as she moved into the darkness.

"Lecramberti caught it head-on as she drove out of the side-road, a heavy lorry," she said in a husky whisper. "Well, that's that. We might as well go home."

"Yes," agreed Grant. "I don't think Herf is here, or ever was. We must wait and contact the others."

Todd came down the road, slowly. Grant stepped out behind the car and Todd drew in.

"Hell of a mess," he said. "I guess she's bought a one way ticket."

A small red lamp on Todd's handle-bars glowed. Todd took up the receiver. "Todd here," he said. "Receiving clear." Grant and Jenny waited, trying to guess what it was. Then Todd reported the accident and signed out.

"Well?" demanded Grant.

"You can go home and brew yourself a nice cup of cocoa. The cops took Herf half an hour ago."

"So?" said Grant, very softly. "Who was that on the air?"

"The Old Man. He sounded as if he was talking with broken glass in his mouth. Oh, boy, I guess he's raving mad that the cops nobbled his pet bug and not us. Between ourselves, I wouldn't call Herf one of our successes."

"What does it matter who got him?" demanded Jenny.

"The Old Man was dead set on knocking off Herf himself. It doesn't matter a tinker's damn to us, maybe. But it does to him. Well, so long. I'll tell Martin and McLellan. Then we'll go and have a nice, foaming pint together. I can do with it. Be good."

Todd swung his motor-cycle in a smooth turn and roared away.

Jenny said: "We ought to see if there's anything we can do for Winifredo Lecramberti. Poor woman! Perhaps she wasn't all that bad."

But there was nothing they could do. When they reached the scene of the accident Winifredo Lecramberti was being loaded on to a stretcher, and they had a cover over her face.

26

DETECTIVE CONSTABLE ROGER ASHBRIDGE
was a bright young man who had joined
the Metropolitan Police with the idea of
getting on. He had not long been transferred from the uniformed branch to the
C.I.D. but up to the present nothing
more exciting than routine jobs had come
his way. After three hours of standing in
shop doorways and loitering in the rain
he was getting frankly bored. Watching
the second-hand furniture shop of Stephan
Morizov was not an inspiring job. Only
one woman customer had gone in, a
woman surprisingly well-dressed for the
neighbourhood. She had come out again
looking rather distressed, he thought. But
she had driven away in her car before
he could make up his mind whether this
was a matter to be reported or not. In the
end he decided it was not important, but
he did record the car number.

Ashbridge moved out of the doorway
and took a slow walk to the corner, where

he hoped he might see the other detective constable on duty with him. He was walking back, thinking about his fiancée and their marriage in April in time to get the benefit of a married man's allowance for income tax, a nice present from the Board of Inland Revenue, when he saw the man in a black coat, collar turned up, and soft, black hat pulled over his eyes go into the second-hand furniture shop. He saw the second man, too, almost the twin of the other, a few yards along the street, standing with his hands in his overcoat pocket.

The young constable dismissed his private affairs from his mind and concentrated on the job. The first man came out of the shop, joined the other, spoke to him for a minute or so, and returned to the shop. The second man began to walk away. He turned into a side street and disappeared.

Ashbridge stepped into the doorway opposite and used his neat little walkie-talkie set, the latest invention in portable radio. When he made contact he reported what he had seen and was told to wait, a patrol car would bring further orders.

It was then that Ashbridge observed another man on the opposite pavement, looking into the shop. He was a big man, clad in a heavy overcoat and dark grey hat. Ashbridge felt a sudden little thrill of excitement. He was almost certain this was the man for whom he was watching. When the man moved on down the street Ashbridge eased out from his hiding place and followed. At the corner the man turned into the narrow street leading off the main road. Ashbridge was about to follow when he saw his colleague crossing the road. Detective Constable Barber had recognized him, too. Ashbridge dodged through the traffic and came up behind Barber, following him. They had been warned that the man would be armed and prepared to shoot.

Leading off the street was an alley with a street light at the end. Ashbridge saw the man pass under the light and turn into the alley. Barber checked and moved up slowly. He turned as he heard Ashbridge.

"That's Peter Herf," he said. "He's gone in the back way to the furniture shop. What do we do? Call up H.Q., or take him ourselves?"

"I've just been told to wait for a patrol car," said Ashbridge. "But I'm game to try it alone. We could always plead urgency."

"Come on then," said Barber. "I'm browned off with watching for a man who wasn't likely to come at all. Now he's here, let's have fun."

The two constables went down the alley. They found the rear doors of the yard open and moved in silently. Before them was a well of darkness from which the building rose in shadowy gloom. A light showed in a single window, high up, throwing a feeble haze on a fire-escape.

At the top of the escape they saw a darker shadow move for a brief moment.

"There he is," whispered Ashbridge. "One of us ought to go in below and the other go up."

"If we can get in," said Barber.

The only door into the rear of the building was locked. Barber tried his shoulder against it, but it was a stout door and would take a lot of breaking in.

"Start climbing," he said. "Maybe we can get in on the way."

On the first floor a window was unlatched. Barber opened it. The room beyond was as dark as a coal mine. He switched on his torch and took a quick look. It was stacked with lumber and old furniture.

"All right," he said. "Go up slowly. Give me time. Watch your step. He's supposed to be armed and dangerous."

Ashbridge began to ascend the iron steps. He was on the last turn when he heard what sounded like pistol shots, muffled, inside the house. He was about to go on, more quickly, when the feeble light above him suddenly became brighter and he heard the clatter of feet on iron.

He looked up and saw the big man like a great, bulky shadow coming down the escape. Ashbridge flattened himself against the side, so as not to be carried down by the sheer weight of the other.

"Hold it," he bellowed. "I am a police officer."

The man came down in a rush. Ashbridge saw the red eye of flame stab in the gloom and heard the vicious ping of the bullet as it struck the iron railing. Then the man was on him, brushing him aside, bearing him down. Ashbridge, on his knees, grabbed at the man's ankles as he passed, and wrenched. It was almost an automatic action, to prevent the other from escaping.

The big man pitched forward, lost his footing, and shot out into empty air. His hand made a frantic grab at the wet, slippery rail, failed to get hold, and fell at his side as he plunged down, straight on to the stone-paved yard, forty feet below.

Ashbridge felt suddenly very sick. But he conquered the urge to vomit and went slowly down. Barber came out on the next floor platform.

"What's happened?" he demanded.

"He fell off the escape," said Ashbridge.

"Somewhere in the distance a police whistle shrilled. The police had arrived in force.

"You go up and find out what's going on above," said Ashbridge. "I'll go down and see if he's alive."

"What a hope!" shrugged Barber. "All right."

Barber went up and Ashbridge went down. Ashbridge found Herf in the centre of the yard. He had pitched on his head and it wasn't a pretty sight when Ashbridge shone his torch. He couldn't conquer the nausea any longer and he was violently sick. He was still being sick when a patrol sergeant and two men came into the yard.

"Who's this?" demanded the sergeant, shining his torch on the dead man.

"Peter Herf, Sergeant. He fell from the top floor."

"What a bit of luck!" said the sergeant. "Better let him stay until the Super arrives. Anyone else copped it?"

"There were pistol shots. Barber is up there."

The sergeant began to mount the steps, the two constables following. Ashbridge was left along with the body. He wondered if he ought to tell the exact truth as to how Herf had died. He thought not. The super would ask so many damned questions as to why he had grabbed him by the ankle when he must have known it would result in the prisoner's death. Well, he hadn't known. He hadn't thought about it. He'd just grabbed. All the same, it wasn't a happy thought that he had been responsible for another man's death, even if he was a murdering hound who had tried to kill him.

Two men in plain clothes came into the yard. Ashbridge challenged them with sharp authority.

"All right, Constable," said the taller man. "I am Chief Superintendent Bellamy. Tell me how it happened."

Ashbridge told him, all of it, the truth.

"Good work, Ashbridge," said Bellamy. That made it all right for Ashbridge. "Have you searched him?"

"No, sir."

Bellamy turned to his companion.

"Perhaps you would prefer to do it, Colonel."

Ashbridge wondered who the hell the other might be. That he was someone of importance he guessed.

As Colonel Borlaise knelt beside the dead man, Bellamy said: "Hold your torch on him, Ashbridge."

Ashbridge watched as expert hands went over the body. He saw the long envelope brought out from inside the shirt. When the other drew out some papers and studied them by the light of the torch beam he saw the official crest.

Borlaise stood up, thrusting the papers back into the envelope, and slipping it into his coat pocket.

"Yes," he said. "It's what I want. He's got other papers on him, too."

"You'll let them wait?"

"Yes. I'll see them all later. I want the lot, however unimportant they appear to be."

"I'll have them sent over to you," said Bellamy. "Ashbridge, escort this gentleman to his car. I'm going up. Good night, Colonel."

Ashbridge walked with Colonel Borlaise down the side street to the main road. There were two police cars parked outside the shop and between them was the car he had seen before. He recognized the girl, too. She looked even more worried than she did before.

"Do you know her?" demanded Borlaise.

"No, sir. But the same girl was here about an hour ago. She went into the shop and came out again. She looked worried, I thought."

"No doubt," said Borlaise. "She'll be more worried still before long. Well, thank you, Ashbridge. You don't know it, but you've done a fine job of work tonight. Don't think too much about it. He wasn't fit to live."

"No, sir. Thank you, sir," said Ashbridge.

27

"WELL THAT'S THE end of Peter Herf. And we have to thank a raw recruit to the C.I.D. for it."

Colonel Borlaise struck a match and lit his pipe. Grant said nothing. There wasn't much that was safe to say when the Old Man was in his present mood.

"We put up a poor show, Grant. I'm not blaming you, or anyone. Only myself. I had information you did not. Well, never mind. We have those damned documents and we know we shall have no more headaches from Herf. Let's be satisfied."

"Why did Herf go to Morizov's shop?" asked Grant. "He must have been desperate to take that chance."

"Because he thought Morizov could still be made to obey him. He knew how to get into the premises by the fire escape. He counted on not being seen. But he picked a bad time. There was a Polish security man with Morizov, working on him to get the truth. The Pole was as quick with a gun as Herf. They shot together. The Pole was hit in the arm, but Herf was not. Herf bolted, probably suspecting there were more Poles in the house."

"And the girl, sir?" The one who came to drive Herf to Norfolk."

"That, Grant, was Mollie Van Dansen, one of Morgan Porthy's models for his photographs. Remember, you brought a copy of one to me?"

"Indeed I do, sir. Will she be charged?"

"No. What purpose would it serve? The little fool has got herself mixed up with the damned Communist Party. She says Herf telephoned her to meet him at Morizov's shop, saying he wanted her to drive him to Norfolk, and make excuses to her father if she had any other engagements. She seems to have been in love with Herf. And she declares she thought she was obeying orders from the Party. I'll have to warn her father. He'll have her back in Holland immediately. He can't afford to have a stupid daughter like that running loose. Well, Van Dansen hasn't been as reasonable as he might have been

In future he'll be more co-operative."

"I suppose Hemmer will be charged, sir?"

"You can be sure of that. Hemmer is a damned, dirty traitor. In war time he'd be shot. As it is, he'll go down for ten years, at least."

"And the other?"

Borlaise made a violent gesture of disgust.

"That damned pansy! The Americans want him."

"For espionage?"

"Yes. He's an American subject. They can have him."

"Was he working with Herf?"

"He doesn't admit it, of course, but obviously he was."

"I suppose he and Hemmer were going to meet Herf in France. Hemmer would have lost his microfilm, unless he was going into the racket with them."

"More likely Herf would have shot him. Oh, well, our job is done. You'd better have some leave, Grant."

"I would like to have two months special leave, sir."

"Why?"

"I want to go to the Isles of Hyeres, to have sand, sunshine, and warm water in which to swim. I think it's an ideal place for a honeymoon. Jenny agrees with me."

"I see," said Borlaise. "So I'm to lose Jenny, am I?"

"Jenny would be prepared to continue in her job, sir."

"I don't have married women on my staff, Grant. You know that."

"I'm very glad, sir."

Borlaise stared at him, his cold eyes hard and grim. Then slowly his lips relaxed in a smile. He stood up and held out his hand.

"I knew I'd have to lose her some day," he said. "There is no man I'd rather lose her to than you, Grant."

The Colonel's grip was warm and firm. Grant thought he really meant what he said. It was very flattering. He knew Jenny would be delighted.

THE END

MYSTERY TITLES IN THE ULVERSCROFT LARGE PRINT SERIES

WESTERN TITLES IN THE ULVERSCROFT LARGE PRINT SERIES

The Invisible Outlaw	*Max Brand*
The Trembling Hills	*Norman Fox*
The Devil's Saddle	*Norman Fox*
Lone Star Ranger	*Zane Grey*
The Drift Fence	*Zane Grey*
Sunset Pass	*Zane Grey*
The Hash Knife Outfit	*Zane Grey*
Lynch Town	*John Kilgore*
The Skyliners	*Louis L'Amour*
Hondo	*Louis L'Amour*
Shalako	*Louis L'Amour*
Matagorda	*Louis L'Amour*
Dark Canyon	*Louis L'Amour*
The Empty Land	*Louis L'Amour*
Kilrone	*Louis L'Amour*
Under the Sweetwater Rim	*Louis L'Amour*
The High Graders	*Louis L'Amour*
North to the Rails	*Louis L'Amour*
Tombstone for a Troubleshooter	
	Wm. Colt MacDonald
Trouble at Topaz	*Frank C. Robertson*
The Kean Land	*Jack Schaefer*
Double Cross Ranch	
	Charles Alden Seltzer

Square Deal Sanderson
Charles Alden Seltzer

"Drag" Harlan *Charles Alden Seltzer*

The Boss of the Lazy Y
Charles Alden Seltzer

THE SHADOWS OF THE CROWN TITLES IN THE ULVERSCROFT LARGE PRINT SERIES

King's Adversary   *Monica Beardsworth*
A Call of Trumpets   *Jane Lane*
The Trial of Charles I   *C. V. Wedgwood*
Royal Flush   *Margaret Irwin*
The Sceptre and the Rose   *Doris Leslie*
Mary II: Queen of England

                         Hester Chapman
That Enchantress   *Doris Leslie*
The Princess of Celle   *Jean Plaidy*
Caroline the Queen   *Jean Plaidy*
The Third George   *Jean Plaidy*
The Great Corinthian   *Doris Leslie*
Victoria in the Wings   *Jean Plaidy*
The Captive of Kensington Palace

                            Jean Plaidy
The Queen and Lord 'M'   *Jean Plaidy*
The Queen's Husband   *Jean Plaidy*
The Widow of Windsor   *Jean Plaidy*
Bertie and Alix *Graham & Heather Fisher*
The Duke of Windsor   *Ursula Bloom*

We hope this Large Print edition gives you the pleasure and enjoyment we ourselves experienced in its publication.

There are now over 700 titles available in this ULVERSCROFT Large Print Series. Ask to see a Selection at your nearest library.

The Publisher will be delighted to send you, free of charge, upon request a complete and up-to-date list of all titles available.

Ulverscroft Large Print Books Ltd.,
Station Road, Glenfield,
Leicester, England.